# VOLUME TWO

AIRSHIP 27 PRODUCTIONS

AN AIRSHIP 27 PRODUCTION

Ghost Boy Volume Two

"Orion's Belt" © 2015 Terry Alexander
" Rise of the Atomic Army" © 2015 J. Walt Layne
"Monster from a Nightmare World" © 2015 Erik Franklin
"The Sound of Obedience" © 2015 Lee Houston Jr.

 Published by Airship 27 Productions
www.airship27.com
www.airship27hangar.com

Interior llustrations © 2015 Gary Kato
Cover illustration © 2015 Zachary Brunner

Editor: Ron Fortier
Associate Editor: Gordon Dymowski
Production and design by Rob Davis.

ISBN-13: 978-0692536674 (Airship 27)
ISBN-10: 0692536671

Printed in the United States of America

10 9 8 7 6 5 4 3 2 1

# GHOST BOY
## VOLUME TWO
## TABLE OF CONTENTS

# ORION'S BELT
## BY
## TERRY ALEXANDER

**I**'m leaving, Kid. The Gosling's fueled up and ready." General Jack Munroe tugged his uniform cap on his head. "Take care of things while I'm gone. Captain Jennings will handle the military end." He checked his watch for the tenth time. "I'm not looking forward to the long flight, but Winston was a friend."

"Don't worry, Jack." Alex Conroy leaned on the doorframe and passed him a dog-eared paperback. "You can read this on the trip. Don't worry about things here. POPS and I will be fine for a few days."

"Yes," POPS spoke in a flat monotone voice. "It is proper that you attend the former Prime Minister's funeral. Failure to show the proper respect could cast the United States in a bad light."

"Politics be hanged," Jack snapped. "That's not why I'm going. Winnie was a good man and a friend." He snatched the paperback from Alex's hand. He turned it over and glanced at the lurid cover of a cowboy and an Indian locked in a life or death struggle while a beautiful redhead looked on in terror. "Haven't read this one." He smiled.

"Hopefully you'll find the time to finish it." Alex returned the grin.

"Things have been quiet around here. Why don't you take your girl on that picnic to the Superstition Mountains? You cancelled the last one." He turned toward the door.

"Gilda will like that." Alex fell into step at the older man's side. "She was disappointed when Marto ruined our plans."

"Just be careful in the mountains, Kid." Jack paused at the door.

"General, this is the perfect time of year for an outing in the Arizona wilderness," POPS said. "During the summer the temperature will be well over a hundred degrees."

"It's reached a hundred and fifteen in July and August." Jack nodded. "Just make sure the place is still standing when I return."

"Of course, General." A puzzled tone entered POPS' voice. "The facility will be standing upon your return."

General Munroe grumbled under his breath as he made his way to the waiting aircraft.

Lee Allyn walked across the cold tarmac of O'Hare International Airport toward the waiting Pan Am 707. His vapor breath swirled around his head. He hadn't seen his grandson since his son Brian moved to Florida several months ago. Shirley, his daughter-in-law, said Orin was growing like a weed, the last time he talked with her. Maybe it was his age, but the need to connect with family was vitally important.

He passed under the shadow of the massive wing. Glancing at the line and wishing it would move faster his eyes strayed to the line of passengers disembarking from a TWA flight. He stopped suddenly, jamming the foot traffic. His gaze locked on an attractive blonde walking toward the terminal. Someone jostled Lee from behind; anxious travelers circled him in their haste to reach the plane.

"Hey Mac, get out of the way," a surly man with a wide brimmed hat and a toothpick protruding from his lips snarled.

"Huh, oh sorry," Lee mumbled. *I've seen that woman before, back in the old days.* He turned and walked against the flow of pedestrians, fighting his way back to the boarding gate.

"Hey, Fella, the plane is this way." A heavy woman with thick eyeliner groaned, as he pushed his way through the horde.

*That's Illyria, damn it. I know that's her.* Lee licked his lips nervously.

"Excuse me, Sir," a young, shapely flight attendant grabbed his arm. "We're boarding now. If you've forgotten something, I'll call the desk and have someone bring it to the plane."

"I've changed my mind," Lee stammered. "There's something I've got to take care of." He pulled away from her grasp and ran toward the arrival gate.

His lungs burned as he reached the door. *Haven't done this in a while. I'm getting soft.* Lee drew in a deep breath and moved inside. He circled the area, peering at faces, trying to find Illyria.

"Looking for someone, Mr. Allyn?" a sultry voice whispered in his ear, her arm circled his throat.

He recognized the voice instantly. Lady Illyria, the Queen of Spies.

"Perhaps you saw a familiar face?" her voice heavy with loathing. "You've changed since the war ended. You weren't so careless then. You've gone to seed. Sit this one out old man."

"What's going on here?" A uniformed police officer walked toward them.

"Help me," Lee gurgled, blood rushing to his face, his vision growing cloudy. "Help me!"

The crowd shoved and jostled, gawking at the bizarre scene before them. "This man is ill." The blonde's voice sounded far away. "He approached me and nearly passed out. I caught him to keep him from falling."

"Looks like you're choking him to me." The officer approached cautiously. "Put him in a chair."

She removed her hands, letting the officer struggle with Lee's dead weight. "As you wish." She backed away.

Lee gulped air, slowly taking in his surroundings. Slurred disembodied voices mumbled from the crowd.

"Call an ambulance for Christ sakes."

"Why are you waiting? Get a doctor."

"Yes, get the poor man some help." A heavy-set woman knelt by his side fanning his face with a newspaper.

Illyria disappeared in the confusion.

Lee grew more aware after several minutes. "What is this?" He blinked several times, running his hands through his short cropped salt and pepper hair. "What's going on?"

"It's okay, I think you fainted." The officer grinned.

"Like hell." Lee struggled to his feet, swaying unsteadily. "The blonde woman, where did she go?"

"I lost her in the confusion." The gray haired man placed a restraining hand on Lee's shoulder. "Please sit down. A doctor is on his way here."

"You idiot," Lee snapped. "Forget the doctor. Switch my ticket. I've got to get to Arizona."

"That was very careless." A dark-haired man caught the blonde's elbow. He hurried her to the street. "You nearly ruined our plans."

"That was Lee Allyn. He recognized me." She hurried to match his stride. "He served as a special agent during the war."

"You met him during the war?" He cast her a hard look. "Why did you not inform the KGB?"

"It was a chance meeting. I was undercover. He was an attaché at a diplomatic conference. Truthfully, I'd forgotten he even existed."

"Illyria, the wheels are in motion. Even the slightest mistake could mean failure."

"We will not fail, Ivan." Her eyes swept the street searching for their driver. "We will destroy the SOS," she whispered.

"Can I help you folks?" An elderly man approached. "I can hail you a cab."

"We're waiting for our car," Illyria snapped.

A shiny black sedan rounded the corner and stopped at the curb.

"My word, I've never seen anything like that before." The old man scratched his head. "What kind of car is that?" He reached for their luggage, preparing to load it into the truck.

"Go away." Ivan grabbed his hand and twisted.

The old man grimaced, pain etched across his lined face. "My God, fellah, what's wrong with you?" The old man snatched his hand away.

"Please forgive, Ivan. He's upset, not used to flying." Illyria pulled a fifty dollar bill from her purse and stuffed it in the old man's hand. "Please accept this small token as an apology."

"Sure Lady, anything you say." He backed away slowly, cradling his left arm to his chest.

The driver, a huge man with wide shoulders and a block-shaped head, crawled from the driver's seat and stuffed the bags in the trunk. The two passengers settled into the rear seat as the car sped away.

"You scold me because a man recognized me." Illyria turned to Ivan, anger building to rage. "And then you foolishly attack an old man, and why did your driver use this car? Russian made automobiles aren't common in the United States."

"Gregor, why did you drive this automobile?" Ivan demanded.

"Please forgive me, Comrade." The big man winced at the harsh words. "I am used to this car. I hate American vehicles."

"Idiot, why didn't you simply announce our arrival?" Illyria fumed, staring at Ivan.

"The damage has been done. We must move quickly." Ivan glanced through the windows at the traffic on either side of their vehicle.

"We must change vehicles." Illyria pulled the blonde wig from her head, dumping it on the seat; she ran her fingers through her raven-black hair. "Make arrangements to have the old man eliminated tonight."

"Alex, it's lovely." A wide smile split Gilda's face. "This place hasn't changed since I was a child."

He approached her from behind and slipped his arms around her waist. "That's *Weaver's Needle*, according to the legends the entrance to the *Lost Dutchman's Mine* is at the end of its shadow."

"My Grandpa used to tell me stories of gold seekers when I was a little girl. Hundreds of people have searched for the lost mine." She snuggled closer to his chest. "We should start the picnic. I've got to go to work tomorrow."

"We've got plenty of time. Let's enjoy the view for a few minutes and then we'll eat."

*People hurt, need help.*

Confused, jumbled thoughts seared into Alex's mind. He broke the embrace suddenly, thought lines wrinkled his face.

"Alex." She turned and stroked his cheek. "What's wrong?"

The sound of an approaching car caught his attention.

"Someone's coming," he mumbled.

*Need help. Need water.*

A black and white *Galaxy 500* sporting a red bubble light in the center of the roof came into view. Alex focused a mental probe on the driver.

*Got to find those two today. They'll never survive another night in this wilderness without water.*

The vehicle stopped beside Alex's 63 *Chrysler Newport*. A bleary-eyed officer opened the door, stepped to the ground and straightened his tall frame. "Hello," he plastered a smile on his face to mask his exhaustion. "Deputy Sheriff Louis Pima. An older couple disappeared in these mountains three days ago, Have you seen anyone else up here?"

"I'm Alex Conroy. This is Gilda Jennings. We're having a picnic."

Gilda nodded. "You look exhausted. Would you like a sandwich or something to drink?"

"I'm fine." Pima shook his head. "Have you seen anything out of the ordinary?" he repeated.

Alex recalled the garbled thoughts he'd received earlier. "I thought I saw something moving, west of the needle a couple of minutes ago."

"Frank and Iris Pickford are gold hunters. They both carried a canteen, but even in February the desert gets hot during the day." Pima licked his lips. "I'll walk down there and check things out. Hopefully I'll get lucky and find them."

"That's awful. When I was little, my Mom and Dad used to vacation here." Gilda said. "We stayed in the cabins near *Apache Junction*."

"I remember those cabins. Nate Thompson used to own that place. A couple rented the property from his kids after he died, but they couldn't make a go of things. The place is deserted now."

"I'd like to go with you." Alex stared into Gilda's eyes. "You could wait in the car. We shouldn't be gone more than a couple of hours."

"I could use the help, but the sheriff would have my hide if he found out."

"We won't tell a soul." Alex shook his head.

"Come on. The main rescue party is about three miles from here. We found some strange tracks, and followed them for a half mile, lost the trail on some rocks." Pima pulled a canteen from his vehicle, and slung the strap over his shoulder.

"Have you heard of The Shrieking man?" Gilda folded her hands together; a look of fear marred her comely features.

"You've heard the old stories." Pima settled his hat on his head.

"I saw him once when I was a small girl. That was the last time we vacationed here." Gilda edged toward the *Chrysler.*

"You never told me that story." Alex stared at the needle, mentally searching for the mind he'd discovered earlier.

*Need help, need water.*

Jumbled thoughts filled his mind.

"In the forties, some old timers saw something they couldn't explain and several people found these big huge tracks. In December of 44, twenty-five German sailors escaped from Papago Park."

"The POW camp near Phoenix," Gilda mumbled.

"Yeah," Pima glanced at Alex, a frown wrinkled his face. "A bunch of locals, armed with shotguns, swarmed over the *Superstitions* looking for them. They swear they saw the Shrieking Man. The German's were very eager to surrender. I don't know what they saw, but my Uncle has plaster casts of the footprints." He glanced at Gilda. "Is your boyfriend feeling well?"

"There, I saw it again, a splash of color west of the needle, by that huge mound of rocks." Alex returned Pima's glance. "And I'm fine." He turned to Gilda. "Wait for me in the car. I won't be long."

"Be careful, Alex." She licked her lips.

"I will." He followed the deputy down the well-worn trail.

"I've seen you somewhere before," Pima said. "Where are you from?"

"Gilda lives in Tucson. I work for the military." Alex concentrated trying to maintain contact with the confused thoughts. "There, I saw it again."

"I didn't see anything." Pima scratched his head. "Are you sure you saw something?"

"I'm sure." Alex nodded. "I'll go down there by myself if you want to quit."

"No, I'll go with you." Pima ran a hand across his sleep-weary eyes.

*I've got to get away from this guy. I can fly down there before we cover a quarter of the distance on foot.* His eyes swept their surroundings, searching for any excuse to send the deputy in another direction. To his surprise, Pima found a track, running diagonally across their trail.

"Look at that." He grabbed Alex's sleeve and yanked him to a stop. "That's his track, that's the Shrieking Man's tracks. It's just like the one my Uncle cast years ago."

Alex knelt to examine the large footprints. Eighteen inches long with long thick toes. Alex scratched his head. "I've never seen anything like this before."

"It's traveling southwest, away from the rocks." Pima followed the bizarre prints. "I think we should follow these tracks."

"Deputy, stick with the tracks. I'll go to the rock pile, if I don't find anything I'll go back to the car."

"Don't go anywhere else." Pima glared. "I don't want to be out here looking for you."

"Don't worry about me." Alex smiled. "I can see the car. I won't get lost."

"I don't like splitting up." The deputy bit his lip in indecision. "Go on and I'll meet you back at the vehicle in an hour."

Pima focused his attention on the tracks, Alex turned toward the vehicles. He couldn't see Gilda. A mental probe confirmed that she was in the *Chrysler* anxiously waiting for him to return.

Alex closed his eyes and concentrated. His body faded from view as he lifted from the earth and flew toward his destination. He circled the needle and lowered himself to the ground and turned visible. Moving to the far side of the rocks, he spied an elderly couple lying in the shade of the large boulders.

A heavy weight slammed his back, Alex rolled with the blow. Two unnaturally large hands circled his throat. He grabbed the thumbs and twisted, moving to the side, he hip-tossed the larger attacker to the ground. Ghost Boy spun and assumed a combat stance.

"You devil, appear from air. Not hurt, man and woman." The creature spoke in a thick, guttural voice. It climbed to its feet, standing well over six feet. Threadbare and torn rags covered its hairy body. The face pinched forward, in a canine snout. "Not hurt."

"You can talk," Alex mumbled. "I'm not going to hurt them. The Pickford's need help. They need water and medical attention. I know you don't want to hurt them, let me help."

"You lie. Like other men, you lie to Hideous." The man-beast jumped for his throat.

Alex caught a flashing glimpse of sharp talons, as he turned intangible. The on-rushing monster passed through his incorporeal form.

Alex reappeared behind the beast. "Is that your name, Hideous? Why are you here?"

"Hideous, hide from evil men." He swung at Alex with his claw-tipped hands. "Bad men chase Hideous, try to have him do evil things again. But no more. Hideous not do bad things again."

"I've heard of you. You worked for the mob before the war." Alex backed away from the flurry of blows.

"No more talk. Leave Hideous alone," the brute screamed. "Leave Hideous alone!"

"I won't hurt you." Alex held his arms away from his body. "I want to help the Pickford's. I won't hurt them. I'm not a devil, or an evil man. I just want to help."

Hideous charged. His right arm swept back in a killing blow, the talons aimed for his throat. Alex stood unmoving, staring at the man beast. The clawed hand streaked forward, speeding for his throat.

Hideous stopped his momentum at the last instant, his arm dropped to his side. "Hideous not kill. Take hurt people and go." He turned his back, walking slowly toward a distant peak.

"You were trying to help the Pickford's, you probably saved their lives." Alex walked toward the beast.

The creature stopped.

"How long have you been here?" Alex asked. "How have you survived?"

"Many years," The wide shoulders shrugged. "Eat snakes, lizards, find water in mountains."

"The Pickford's have been missing for three days. A search party is looking for them."

"Hideous go. Help hurt people."

"I want to make you an offer." Alex edged closer. "If you're willing to trust me, I can offer you a place to stay, food and shelter. Just come back with me to the base."

"Hideous no want cage. No people prodding Hideous. No want pain."

"I'm offering you a place to live, a chance to help people."

"Hey, Alex, where are you?" Pima shouted.

"That's the deputy." Alex licked his lips. "I'll send a truck back tonight. It'll have a cover over the bed. If you're interested, crawl inside and my men will drive you to the compound."

"What your name?"

"Alex Conroy."

"Alex." Hideous struggled with the name. "Send truck tonight. Maybe

Hideous go with you." He turned and trotted away, disappearing into the desert.

"Over here, Deputy Pima. I found the Pickford's," Alex yelled. "They need water and a doctor."

"You got here fast." A sweat-soaked Pima ran to the pile of boulders. "I lost sight of you as soon as we split up."

"How far did the tracks go?" Alex asked, changing the subject.

"Two or three hundred yards, then they petered out." Pima pulled a soggy handkerchief from his back pocket and mopped his face. He pulled the canteen from his hip and passed it to Alex. "Give them a sip, if they're able to swallow."

Alex knelt by the woman, lifted her head and held the canteen to her lips. "Can your walkie-talkie reach the other searchers?"

"Yeah." He pulled it from the leather holster on his hip. "Unit two to Sheriff Rollins, Unit two to Sheriff Rollins." A feedback squeal came from the speaker when Pima released the transmission button.

"Rollins here. Any luck, Pima?"

"They're here, close to *Weaver's needle*. Need some help carrying them out."

"I'll radio for an ambulance, should be there in twenty minutes." The walkie went silent.

Alex brushed sandy grit from his hands, he climbed to his feet. "Well, Deputy Pima, things worked out well. I need to be going. I've got to have Gilda home by midnight. She has to work tomorrow."

"Wait a minute. You can't go. Sheriff Rollins will want a statement from you." Pima grabbed his sleeve. "You saved these people. You're a hero."

"Pima." Alex shrugged. "You've been searching for these people for three days. You deserve the credit." Alex turned to leave.

"How am I gonna explain all these tracks?" Pima shouted.

"You'll think of something." Alex winked.

Pima bent to check on the Pickford's. Alex willed himself invisible and rose into the air. Luck proved to be on his side. Gilda paced the ground next to the *Chrysler*, giving him a moment to land behind her and turn visible.

"Good news, we found them," he said.

"Now, can we enjoy our picnic?" she asked, hugging him close.

Alex shook his head. "The sheriff and an ambulance are on the way here. We should leave. The Pickford's aren't out of danger yet."

Lee Allyn stopped at the wire gate leading to the SOS (Scientific Operational Security) compound. A nervous private approached, his rifle slung over his shoulder. *My God,* Lee shook his head. *The kid looks like he graduated high school last week.*

"I'm sorry, Sir," The Private stammered. "You're in a restricted area. You have to turn around and leave."

"General Jack Munroe will skin you alive, if he sees you carrying your weapon like that." Lee grinned. "You should carry your rifle at port arms."

"Sir, I can't speak with you. You have to leave, this is a…"

"I know it's a restricted area, and I need special clearance to get inside." He gazed into the Private's eyes. "Orion's Belt."

The color drained from the young man's face. "What…" he swallowed. "What did you say, Sir?"

"Orion's Belt." The look on the kid's face said it all. Lee chuckled to himself, *twenty years later and Jack still has the same emergency code word.*

"I'll call the OD immediately." The red-faced youth ran to the guard shack.

"Tell General Munroe to have a cold beer waiting for me." Lee chuckled.

"Sir, the general isn't available at the present time." The sentry nervously dialed the phone. "He's flying to England to attend Winston Churchill's funeral."

"Yeah, Winnie was a good man; a real tough bulldog."

Thirty minutes later a pasty faced Lieutenant escorted Lee through the doors into the central hub of the SOS. "If there's anything you need, Mr. Allyn, feel free to call on me."

"What's your name again?" Lee tossed his winter coat on the round table in the center of the huge room. He sleeved sweat from his face and loosened his tie.

"Lieutenant Wilbur, Sir."

"Where is the second in command, doesn't Jack have an aide?"

"Major Jennings will be here shortly. The deputy director is on a picnic, Sir." Wilbur turned his head sheepishly. "The general's last aide resigned after an injury."

Lee shook his head. "Imagine that." He turned to face the young officer. "I was in Chicago this morning, a short plane ride from Florida and my grandkids. Then I saw her on the tarmac, and I knew I had to find Jack."

Heavy metallic footsteps echoed from the walls as POPS entered the room.

"Well," Lee chuckled. "Jack has a robot."

"Actually, Mr. Allyn, I am POPS, short for Photoelectric Optimal Protection Soldier. I was created by David Conroy before his demise."

"Bet you never saw anything like POPS before." The lieutenant smiled.

"Hitler had a small company of robots on the Russian front. A tricky assignment, but I managed to set a trap and blew them to smithereens." Lee met the younger man's gaze. "I worked with the OSS back then, and I reported to Major Jack Munroe."

"Captain Zero, I've read the reports about your assignments during the war. Please consider this as your home. I'll contact Alex immediately and instruct him to return." POPS rushed forward.

"You're more hospitable than Hitler's metal goons." Lee collapsed in the overstuffed chair reserved for General Munroe. "Get Jack on the horn, I saw Lady Illyria in Chicago."

"Who is Lady Illyria?" Lieutenant Wilbur asked.

"Lady Illyria, the Queen of Spies." POPS red vision receptors fastened on the Lieutenant. "She vowed to destroy America during the war. The last intelligence report we received stated she was in Moscow."

"She was with a big dark haired man, wearing a cheap KGB suit." Lee nodded. "Where does Jack keep his beer?"

"I'll find a cold brew for you, Sir." Wilbur turned toward the door.

"I'll get word to General Munroe and Alex." POPS turned to leave.

"Get me a line to the White House. I've got to warn Lyndon." Lee leaned back in the plush chair and closed his eyes. "Where's my beer?"

"Right behind you, Sir." The red-faced officer rushed through the door, an open bottle, covered with condensation drops clutched in his hand.

Lee snatched the brew from his hand. "You two quit dragging your feet, get on the phones. I've got to speak to Lyndon."

The Gosling touched down at *RAF Lakenheath,* a joint United States and Great Britain air base located in *Suffolk.* "These long flights are murder on my back." Jack Munroe growled to the pilot, as he made his way to the side door. He glanced at a dark haired beauty waiting for him on the tarmac, his heart raced wildly, at the sight of her. "Gloria Travers, Ranger Girl, is that really you?" He rushed to her side.

"Hello Jack." She blushed. "I haven't been called Ranger Girl since the war. It's been a long time."

"WELL," LEE CHUCKLED. "JACK HAS A ROBOT."

"Yes, 1949, my last field assignment, before Harry Truman ordered me back to the states. Sorry I couldn't say good-bye. When the orders came through, they escorted me straight to the plane, before I knew it we were in the air." The words rushed from Jack's mouth.

"You could have called after you arrived in the states." Her eyebrows knitted together for an instant. "That's water under the bridge."

"I wish I could stay and relive old times, but I'm supposed to meet my new aide. There's another crisis brewing." Jack shrugged. "It's the story of my life."

"The Vice-President called me two hours ago." Her dark eyes fastened on Jacks face. "We need to talk privately."

"Hubert called you?" A look of confusion covered his face.

"I'm your new aide." She took Jack's arm. "Come on, your vehicle's waiting."

"You're my new aide?" His mouth dropped open in surprise.

"Get in car, Jack." She nodded to the young sergeant who stood by a waiting staff car. "We need to get away from any big ears that might be listening."

Jack opened the rear door and allowed Gloria to slide across the cloth seat. He ducked his head and followed her inside. A light crackle of static played on the radio. Jack knew it played havoc with any listening devices planted inside. He slammed the door behind him. "Lee Allyn saw Illyria in Chicago this morning. POPS didn't provide me with details, so you'll have to bring me up to speed. I thought Lady Illyria was in Russia."

Gloria nodded. "She relocated there after the war, but she hasn't forgotten her vow to destroy the United States. James Perkins had been keeping tabs on her. In his last transmission, he reported that Illyria had a meeting with a high placed official in *SMERSH*."

"Any idea who she met?" Jack ran his stubby fingers through his short cropped hair.

Gloria shook her head. "Perkins was trying to relay the information when he was killed, three bullets to the back of the head." She paused for a moment. "From Lee's description of the man, she's traveling with Ivan Kantorovich."

"Kantorovich, I thought he was dead." Jack tugged a cigar from his pocket, and peeled the wrapping away.

"Don't smoke that foul smelling thing in here," Gloria snapped. "You can light up when we arrive at your temporary quarters."

"A good smoke helps me think," Jack protested.

"Jack, you've always smoked the most rancid cigars. You don't have a clue what a fine cigar really is." Gloria shook her head. "You've dealt with Kantorovich before."

"Ivan is a killer, learned his craft during the war and he enjoys it. The Soviets trained him well." Jack nodded. "If he's involved, the Russians want someone dead. It's a wonder they didn't kill Lee when he recognized Illyria."

"She tried. They were in a crowd and a police officer was watching. Otherwise she would have killed him on the spot." She pointed to a large house, sitting in a far corner of the base. "This is the VIP housing unit. You'll be staying here."

A few moments later the driver braked to a stop in the circular driveway.

"Nice place, little pompous for my taste, but, it'll work." Jack climbed from the vehicle and held the door for Gloria.

"Sergeant, return this vehicle to the motor pool and take the rest of the evening off. I'll expect you here early in the morning." Gloria nodded to the soldier.

"Yes, Sir," He saluted the general. "I'll be here at 0600."

"Good man." Jack returned the salute. "I'll be ready." He turned to Gloria, as the car drove away. "Is this place secure?"

"I've gone over it twice. It's clean." She pulled a key from her purse and unlocked the door. They stepped inside and Gloria reached out and flipped the wall switch. Brilliant light flooded the large living room. A bizarre looking woman, her face hidden by a wide hat, sat on the sofa. A *Walther P-38* gripped tightly in her fist, centered on the General's middle.

"Good evening, General." The female spoke in a sultry voice. "I've been expecting you. Please shut the door behind you."

Alex burst through the door, his face flushed with excitement. "POPS, find Lieutenant Wilbur. I need an enclosed truck at *Weaver's Needle* before midnight."

"Alex, we have an emergency." POPS said in a dry emotionless voice.

"The picnic was a disaster. Gilda's upset. I'll send her flowers, maybe some candy." He turned to the strange man sitting at the conference table. "Oh, excuse me. I'm Alex Conroy. I didn't mean to be rude."

"Alex," POPS interrupted. "This is Lee Allyn, Captain Zero. He has grave news. Another of General Munroe's old enemies has resurfaced."

"Not again." Alex flopped into his customary chair. "Who is it this time?"

"Illyria." Lee locked eyes with Alex.

"What?" The color drained from Alex's face.

"Lady Illyria, the Queen of Spies, saw her in Chicago this morning. I don't know how many of Jack's enemies you've faced, but let me tell you this threat is real, Illyria is dangerous and she's not alone."

"I'm sorry. I've got a lot of things on my mind." Alex nodded.

"I had girlfriend problems in the past myself, goes with the job." Lee agreed. "But you need to get your head in the game. Jack's gone. You have to make the decisions until he returns."

"You're right." He turned to the mechanical man. "POPS, find Lieutenant Wilbur. Tell him to drive a transport to *Weavers Needle* and wait for a passenger to get in the back."

"That's a very unusual request." The robot's red orbs fastened on the young man. "Who are we transporting?"

"Tell him to drive to the needle and wait inside the truck. If I'm right our passenger will climb in the back. Oh, make sure the truck is enclosed," Alex said.

"Alex, this is very irregular."

"It'll be worth it." He turned to Lee. "You've had experience with Lady Illyria?"

"She worked for the Axis during the war. Came close to killing me a couple of times. I've got a scar running from my hip to my knee and some shrapnel in my leg from her last caper." Lee patted his right thigh.

"According to Army Intelligence, she's working for the Soviets."

Lee nodded. "An inside man was keeping track of her. He was murdered. From my description, the bright boys in intelligence identified her traveling companion as Ivan Kantorovich."

"I've heard that name before." A frown creased Alex's face.

"Kantorovich is an assassin for *Smersh*. Rumors are, he was killed by Starr Flagg in the Ural Mountains in 1959," POPS said.

"That's it, Dyatlav Pass. Nine people were killed in the Ural Mountains." Alex stared at Lee. "Starr was there?"

"Kantorovich nearly killed her. I came out of retirement, Jack and I went into that God-forsaken place and brought her out. She nearly died twice, but we managed to get her to the hospital in Fairbanks." Lee stared through the open window at the lengthening shadows; an involuntary shudder shook his frame. "She stayed in the hospital for eight months, resigned from the service when she was released and got married a year later. She'd love to have another crack at Kantorovich."

"She helped us on a case a few months ago, Starr can still handle herself." Alex nodded.

"I've tried to contact Miss Flagg," POPS said. "No one answered the phone."

"Alex, we received a peculiar message from Fort Bliss." A red-faced, Lieutenant Wilbur raced into the room. "An unidentified aircraft crossed the border into New Mexico, flying north."

"Did the commander scramble intercept planes?" Alex asked.

"Yes." Wilbur nodded. "They lost it. The pilot swore it just vanished from sight. Radar operator said the blip was there one second and gone the next."

Lee jumped to his feet. "Project Vorwand, Smokescreen. Did he get a look at the plane before it disappeared?"

"Dark red, with what appeared to be a swastika on the tail." Wilbur released a deep breath.

"Baroness Blood flew a fighter like that during the war. She dropped out of sight after Germany surrendered, been hiding out in South America for years." Lee glanced at Alex. "You can bet she's tied in with Illyria."

"What are they after?"

"That's obvious. Jack's out of the country and they want to see if you have what it takes to stop them."

"Find O'Neal, I need his experience on this case." Alex turned to POPS.

"Agent O'Neal hasn't finished his training," The robot said in a flat voice.

"He spent years with the FBI. He'll be fine." Alex turned to Lee. "Anything else you can tell me?"

"I talked to the baggage handlers before I left. An old guy had a run-in with our guests. They drove a strange black car. From his description I think it was a *Volga*."

"Can't be many of those on the streets. At least that gives us a place to start. Contact Director Hoover, we need as many men as he can make available. They have to find that car." Alex glanced toward the robot. "When Wilbur returns, have him get his gear ready. He's going to New Mexico with O'Neal."

"Your hireling shouldn't have driven the *Volga* to the airport." Illyria glanced through the right side window. Her gaze settled on row after row of small brick-sided storefronts. "Thankfully, we were able to acquire this automobile without too much fuss."

Kantorovich stared at the Queen of Spies. "The police will find the bodies within two days. All we have accomplished is buying ourselves some time. The Kremlin expects results, Illyria. They will not accept failure."

"I will not fail." She pulled a cigarette from her purse and inserted the tip into an elegant ivory holder. "I have planned everything down to the last detail. We will succeed. We will kill Ghost Boy."

"And the untimely arrival of Captain Zero, was that part of your plan?"

"Coincidence, nothing more." She expelled twin columns of smoke from her nostrils. "I should have killed him."

"That would have been foolish. The police officer was watching too closely. By now, the good captain has alerted the authorities. They will be searching for us." Kantorovich waved the smoke from his face and opened the window.

"Baroness Blood will cross the border into the United States, with our strike force. The American military is testing a nuclear weapon on February the fourth. We will attack the air force base in Nevada." She pulled the cigarette butt from the holder and tossed it out the window. "You packed the special rifle, carefully? I don't want it damaged."

"The weapon is safe." Kantorovich nodded. "The idea of hiring Nazis to participate in this assignment is distasteful to me. I don't trust them."

"You won't deal with the Germans. They're desperate for funds to run their camps in the South America jungle. If they knew you were involved, they would refuse to participate, no matter what we paid them." Illyria smiled. "Some of them hate you far more than they hate Jack Munroe. They feel your race is *Unbermenschen,* Subhuman."

"I am well aware of the word's meaning. I only regret that I didn't kill more Nazis during the war. I remember the seize of Stalingrad, and the cruelty they showed to the Russian people." Kantorovich eyebrows knotted, his face reddened, his hard gaze fastened on the beautiful woman in the seat beside him. "If it were in my power, I would kill them all."

"That is why you will have no contact with the Nazis, your hatred is uncontrollable. Your lack of control could ruin our plans." Her eyes glinted with an evil sparkle. "The Germans will attack the Nevada Proving Grounds on the second. During the battle, we will murder Alex Conroy and the blame will rest on the Nazis who are hiding in South America. While the United States is focused on ferreting them from concealment, we will escape."

"Then we will celebrate the failure of Operation Whetstone." Kantorovich smiled. "Hopefully, I will be allowed the pleasure of killing more Germans."

"Perhaps, but that is not the mission. This is the first strike in my plan to destroy the United States." She pulled a second cigarette from her purse, slipping it into the holder. "When the government of America lies in ruins, then I will celebrate my victory."

"Bunny, is that you?" Jack raised his hands and toed the door shut behind him. "I haven't seen you since that Canadian scam in 61." He stared at the white-haired woman, her pale skin offset by the brilliant blue dress and the dark glasses covering her eyes.

"You know her?" Gloria reached inside her purse.

"Pull that .32 and I'll kill you before you can use it." Bunny centered her pistol on Gloria's chest.

"Bunny used to work with Mista. She's an albino." He pulled Gloria's handbag from her shoulder and tossed it on the couch. "What are you doing in England?"

"Looking for you. I knew you'd come to Churchill's funeral." Bunny placed her weapon on the coffee table in front of the couch. "I've lived in France since 61, got a little night club there. Last week I had a visitor, one you know well."

"Really, which one?" He shrugged.

"Why are we talking to her, there's two of us. We can take her down easy." Anger flashed in Gloria's eyes.

Jack held up a hand for silence. "Give her a minute."

"Von Tug." She met Jack's eyes. "He walked into my place wearing an overcoat with his left hand jammed inside the pocket. The hat he wore couldn't conceal his scarred mug."

"The Vulture's Claw." Jack scratched his day's growth of whiskers.

"He tried to hire me for a job in the states. I told him I wasn't interested. He didn't give me any details, but you know he's up to no good."

"Thanks, Bunny." Jack nodded. "I know the risk you took in coming here. I won't forget it."

She removed her sunglasses and stared at Gloria. Ranger Girl stiffened; a blank look entered her eyes. "She won't remember I was here."

"What about me?"

"I owed you one, Jack." She climbed to her feet showing a great set of legs. "We're even now. I've given up the old ways. I want you to know that. I've got a good life, and I'm not going to ruin it."

"Appreciate the warning."

"We both know the Claw isn't the brains behind this deal," she said. "He's just hired muscle, but he's dangerous. Get your people ready." The large brimmed hat settled on her head. "I hope you can stop them."

"He's working for Illyria." Jack bent and kissed her lightly on the cheek.

"Be on your toes then. That woman hates you," Her hips swayed, as she walked to the door. "Good Luck, Jack." Her pasty-white face split in a big smile. "Your friend will snap out of her trance in a few minutes." Her hand settled on the knob.

"Take care, Jack." She turned the brass knob and disappeared.

"Illyria and the Vulture's Claw, those two are bad news." Jack walked to the kitchen and checked the fridge. "English beer," he mumbled. "Well any port in a storm."

"Who are you talking to?" Gloria demanded. "And how did you get to the kitchen?"

"I walked naturally." He pulled a bottle from the shelf and rummaged through the cabinets for an opener. "Get me a secure line. I've got to talk to Alex."

"It'll take a few minutes." Frown lines appeared on Gloria's forehead. "What just happened?"

"Get the phone and I'll tell you everything." He opened the bottle. "I'm going to sit down and enjoy this beer."

"Lieutenant Wilbur has returned. Your guest is in the rear of the truck," POPS said.

"Good, I'm glad he accepted my offer." Alex rose and walked to the window, watching as the truck backed to the loading dock. "POPS, this guy is weird. We'll have to take it easy with him until he makes the adjustment to the base."

"Who's in there?" Lee placed an empty bottle on the table.

"Found him out in the desert. He disappeared before the war started." Alex walked to the door. The olive drab truck came to a stop. Alex pulled back the tarpaulin. "It's okay. You'll be safe."

"Who is in there?" Lee repeated.

"You've met him before," Alex said. "Come on, Hideous. No one is going to hurt you."

"Hideous, you've brought that monster here?" Lee smashed the bottle on the table, leaving a sharp stabbing weapon in his hand. "Wish I had my .45. I'd kill that mongrel."

The man-monster bounded from the rear of the truck, his large feet and thick leg muscles propelled him through the air. "Hideous know you, remember you. You disappear at night."

"You brought a killer into your facility." Lee swung the makeshift weapon at the man-sized jumping jack. Hideous dodged the blow easily.

"Stop this," Alex yelled. "Break it up. We're not going to have a brawl here."

"You don't want him around. He'll strangle you in your sleep." Lee threw the bottle at the bouncing figure.

"He's a guest here, Lee, same as you, and I expect you both to be civil. I promised Jack we wouldn't wreck the place." Alex positioned himself between Captain Zero and the monster.

Hideous landed in the center of the table, his bent knees absorbed the shock. He hoped to the floor and advanced on Lee Allyn.

"Hideous, not like you. You not good man." His chest bumped Alex's outstretched hand.

"I'm not a murderer," Lee shouted. "When you disappeared, I assumed you died, see I was wrong."

"Please, Mr. Hideous." POPS walked into the room. Quickly analyzing the situation, he moved toward the man beast. "Please, come with me. You must be starving. Would you care for something to drink?"

"Food nice, water good." He followed the robot into the other room. "Not have food in two days."

"Why did you bring him here?" Lee shook his head. "He murdered people in the thirties, he's dangerous."

Alex guided the older man back to the table and Jack's chair. "He's been in the desert for nearly thirty years. I've read the file. He was an enforcer for a mob boss. They took advantage of his limited intelligence, but he's still human and he deserves to be treated as one."

"He's more animal than you realize." Lee glared at the younger man. "I'm gonna keep my eyes on him. If he tries anything, I'll settle his hash for sure."

POPS returned to the conference room. "Our guest is eating now, although, I can't say much for his table manners." He turned to Alex. "You have a call from General Munroe. The operator is switching it here."

The shrill jangle of the phone punctuated POPS' sentence. Alex caught it on the second ring.

"Hang on Jack, I'm gonna put you on speaker." Alex pressed a square button beside the dial. "Go ahead."

"Is Lee with you?" Jack's gruff voice echoed through the room.

"Yeah, Jack, I'm here."

"Remember Bunny?"

"Yeah, Albino Girl, worked with a two-bit crook named Mista," Lee answered.

"She paid me a visit tonight." A long pause followed. "The Vulture's Claw went to her place a few days ago and offered her a job in the states. You can bet he's working for Illyria."

"Jack, we had a communication a little while ago from Fort Bliss. A red plane crossed the border. It had a swastika on the tail," Alex interrupted. "Lee's convinced it's Baroness Blood."

"Damn," Jack cursed. "Who's working the case?"

"Hoover's boys are searching for the *Volga* that met Illyria at the airport, and I'm sending O'Neal and Wilbur to Bliss to track down the plane."

"Sounds like you have everything covered," Jack paused for a second time. "Wish I knew where they're going to strike. I don't think they'll attack the SOS directly, but you never know."

"Hey, Jack, the kid needs to tell you about a new guest he brought in today," Lee said.

"What's he talking about, Alex?" Jack demanded. "What guest?"

Alex exhaled a long breath. "I found Hideous out in the desert. He's been hiding there for years. He looks bad, Jack. He can use our help."

"Hideous is a killer," Jack said.

"I know," Alex confessed. "Jack, I think I can reason with him. I don't think he's dangerous any longer."

"I'll let you make the call on him. I want the SOS on full alert. Triple the armed guards on the perimeter, and put two guards on Hideous. If he tries anything, they're ordered to shoot to kill. Are we clear on that?"

"Yes, General."

"Keep me informed. I'll return after the funeral." The connection severed sharply.

"Thanks, Lee." Alex snapped. "You could have let me tell Jack in my own way and at my choosing."

"He had to know, kid. He's the one responsible for this outfit" Lee shrugged. "Being the man in charge isn't an easy thing."

: : :
: : :

Illyria walked through the doors of a large warehouse on the outskirts of Carlsbad, New Mexico. She glanced at the footprints in the fresh grit covering the cracked concrete, sensed the hateful glares directed her way. "Come out. I've come to talk."

"You're late." A tall blonde woman wearing a form fitting scarlet outfit stepped from the shadows. "We were beginning to think you weren't coming."

Illyria turned to face Baroness Blood, catching a faint glimpse of Von Tug's scarred features. "Where are the others?" she demanded.

"Undercover Girl shot Keitel in the head at point blank range. His wound became infected. He won't be of any help on this mission." Von Tug's raspy voice came from the shadows.

"Where is the Mize girl? Were you able to locate her?" Illyria pulled a handkerchief from her purse and wiped perspiration from her forehead. She stared at the *Mauser* that suddenly appeared in the Baroness' hand.

"Don't make sudden moves. I could have killed you," she snarled, running a hand through her hair. "Tina stepped out for some fresh air. I'm tired of this hot warehouse. I need a bath and a change of clothes."

"No one was supposed to leave here." Illyria snapped. "Everyone had orders to stay hidden until I gave you the details of the assignment."

"Tell us the plan. We'll inform the girl when she returns." Von Tug stepped forward. The light reflected from his scarred, puckered face.

"The plan is simple. The United States military is conducting a nuclear experiment at the Nevada Proving Grounds on the fourth. We will steal the device on the second and use it to destroy the SOS." Illyria's fisted hands settled on her hips. "You three will attack the base; I will use your attack as a diversion and steal the device. You will return here to receive payment. I will use the bomb to destroy Jack Munroe's facility."

"You think that will be easy," Baroness Blood scoffed. "Our plane was spotted when we crossed the border."

"Why hire us?" Von Tug advanced closer, showing Illyria the three digit claw at the end of his left hand. "Last I heard you were working for the soviets."

"I worked for the Russians. They paid very well. I am using that money to fund this mission. If we can destroy the SOS, the United States will fall." Illyria pulled a pack of cigarettes from her purse. She stuffed one in her holder, placed it between her lips, struck a match, and puffed it to life. "If the two of you are afraid to work with me, I can find others."

"It's too late for that and you know it." The Baroness moved to Von Tug's side. "We accept the assignment, but our price has doubled."

"That's impossible." Twin columns of smoke shot from Illyria's nostrils. "I can't afford to pay you more."

"Maybe you should ask your Russian friends for the rest. We are not fools." Von Tug slipped his arm around Baroness Blood's waist and pulled her close. "Double our fee or we're out."

A wide evil smile stretched the Baroness' face. "This is our final contract. We'll take our money and buy an estate in South America."

"And raise many children and live happily ever after, no doubt." Illyria took a final drag of the cigarette, pulled it from the holder, and tossed it aside. "It doesn't work that way with us. We die violently, either by knife or gun, but violently."

"Nice speech," Tina stalked through the overhead door, a man-sized bundle draped over her shoulder. "Who is this?" She threw the limp Russian to the floor.

"No need to ask." Von Tug walked to the helpless man. His foot settled on the intruder's chest and pinned him to the gritty surface. "This is Ivan Kantorovich, a Russian sniper during the war. He killed over three hundred loyal German's."

Kantorovich wiped a stream of blood from his lip. "Twelve more and I would have had four hundred."

"Where did you find him?" Baroness Blood turned to Illyria, her face flushed with anger.

"Five hundred yards from here. He was studying the warehouse with these." Tina tossed a pair of binoculars to Von Tug. "At twelve feet, I pack quite a punch. He never had a chance to fight back."

"You'll not take me so easily again." Kantorovich pushed the heavy boot from his chest. He sat on the concrete floor, ran his fingers through his mussed hair and adjusted his tie.

"You are working for the Soviets," the Baroness screamed, spittle flew from her lips. "You brought a Russian into this operation."

"The Reich is destroyed. You live like vermin, exiled from your own country," Illyria snapped. "I chose to work for the Russians. They have money and resources. The Reich has nothing. The SS stole millions, gold,

"WE ACCEPT THE ASSIGNMENT, BUT OUR PRICE HAS DOUBLED."

art treasures, but we can't access any of this wealth." She stared at each one in turn.

"I had two open avenues after the war, escape to South America or work for the Soviets." She helped the sniper to his feet. "I chose Russia, and it wasn't easy to survive there. It took years to gain a position of trust, years for the Kremlin leadership to trust me with more than basic assignments." She turned to the dark haired man. "Bring the car around."

Kantorovich moved toward the door. No one made a move to stop him.

"I hate America and everything this decadent country represents. We have an opportunity to strike a blow that will ultimately lead to its downfall." She braced her feet wide apart, fisted hands settled on her hips. "I hoped to keep the involvement of the Russians from you. They are providing the funding for this operation. If you join me, each of you will have enough money to live in luxury instead of surviving on scraps. The choice is yours."

"I detest the Soviets." Tina shrank to her normal height. "When our powers began to manifest themselves the Communist's hunted us like animals. We were hiding from them, when we found Marto and nursed him back to health." Her sad eyes fastened on Illyria. "My sister is rotting in a prison cell. If you promise to help me free her, then I'll work with you, even if it means having to tolerate Kantorovich."

"You have my word. Your sister will be free." Illyria smiled.

"We want money." A glare of defiance entered Baroness Blood's eyes. "Triple the original agreement, and if your dog does anything suspicious we'll kill him."

Illyria nodded. "It is a steep price to pay, but I'm willing to bankrupt my future to see this operation succeed. However, I can't raise that amount on short notice. It will be available after the operation is finished." She turned to leave. "Here is a map. Your target is within the red circle. I will meet you there with final instructions. Be prepared to leave in the morning."

"If you deceive us." The Baroness holstered the pistol, and snapped the flap. "I'll scour the earth until I find you, and when I do your death will be long in coming."

"We will serve you well, Lady Illyria," Von Tug laughed.

She walked slowly to the waiting *Cadillac,* confident in the knowledge that Von Tug's lecherous eyes followed every sway of her hips. She added extra emphasis to her natural movements hoping to excite the Vulture's Claw and fan the fires of jealous with The Baroness.

She opened the door and climbed in the rear seat. "Take us to the motel, I need to cleanse the foulness from my body."

"You're going to pay those vermin?" A look of disgust creased the Russian's face. "They are common criminals, murderers."

"That group is far from common. We are more like them than you wish to admit." She pulled a cigarette from her purse and inserted it into the holder and puffed it to life. "We are all murderers, save perhaps the girl. She actually believes we're going to help her free her sister."

"Then she's a fool." Kantorovich shook his head.

"She's desperate, willing to deal with the devil to get what she wants." Illyria drew smoke deeply into her lungs and released it slowly. "Don't worry about the money. They won't live long enough to spend it."

"They suspect nothing of our true plan?"

"They are suspicious, but they are also desperate." She gazed through the window; the setting sun cast long shadows across the ground. "Keep your eyes on them. They'll try to kill you." A lustful smile crossed her face.

"That vixen hypnotized me and you let her walk away." Gloria's cheeks flushed red. "Why?"

"Don't jump to conclusions." Jack shook his head. "Bunny walked away from her old ways, and I didn't do anything I'm ashamed of. That's why I let the kid make the call on Hideous."

"How many women have you known in your lifetime?"

"What difference does that make?" Jack frowned.

Gloria shook her head. "I'm sorry Jack. I remember what we had during the war." Tears misted her eyes. "After Barkley and Cal were killed on the Malay Peninsula, I wanted to die myself. I wouldn't have survived without you." She wiped the salty drops away. "I can do this job. Jack. You know I can."

"I don't know, we may be too close." He exhaled a deep breath.

"Sometimes I think about what might have been, and it doesn't seem fair. We could have been happy together." She closed her eyes for a brief moment.

"But that time is gone forever. I'll pack the jealousy away." She stared into Jack's eyes. "

"Alright." He pulled a cheap cigar from his pocket and fired it to life. "Hope you can cut the mustard." A wreath of thick smoke surrounded his head. "Come on, I want to see the town before the funeral."

"I'm gonna hit the sack." Lee climbed to his feet, and yawned. "This has been a long day, and I'm not as young as I used to be. Where do I bunk?"

"In the room next to Hideous." Alex licked his lips anxiously.

"Give me a pistol," Lee said. ".45 with a full magazine."

"I have a guard on his room. He won't do anything. He gave me his word," Alex argued.

"I want a pistol." Lee folded his arms across his chest.

"I'll give you something better." Alex jumped to his feet, and crossed the room. He pressed a darkish spot on the windowsill. A section of the wall slid toward the ceiling revealing a hidden arsenal. Reaching inside he removed an over-sized pistol. "This is a pulse gun. It can take anyone down." Alex turned and handed the weapon to Lee. "Be careful with it."

"Thanks, Kid." Lee's hand circled the rubber hand grip.

A distinct buzz came from the wrist communicator. Alex pressed a side button and lifted his hand near his lips. "O'Neal, what's the situation?"

"We're here." A disembodied voice squawked through the speaker. "We've talked to the pilot that spotted the red plane. He only caught a glimpse of the aircraft heading north. Wilbur found an old couple that saw a red plane flying low close to Carlsbad. We'll see what we can find. Hopefully, it won't be a wild goose chase."

"Anything I can do for you on this end?" Alex asked.

"No, I'll contact you if we find anything," O'Neal stated.

"Use your head, don't take any unnecessary risks." Alex pressed the button for a second time, severing the connection.

"That's amazing." Lee shook his head. "Looks just like a wristwatch. Wish these things were around in my day." He rose from the chair and stretched. "Wake me up early. I want to shower before breakfast."

Alex waited until Lee disappeared from sight. "POPS."

The robot moved quietly into the room. "Yes, Alex."

"Go through every message we've received in the sixty days. I want to know everything the military has planned for the rest of the week." He stared at the metal man. "My gut is telling me that Illyria and her associates won't wait long. They'll make their move soon."

"That is sound thinking." POPS nodded.

Alex ran a hand through his hair. "I hope I didn't make a serious mistake in bringing Hideous here."

"You did take a great risk," the robot agreed, "but you have good instincts about people. Trust them." POPS turned toward the door. "I will go through all of our communications. When you wake in the morning, I will have an answer."

"I'm not sure this is a good idea," Lieutenant Wilbur whispered. "You're taking a big leap of faith that the old codger in the bar really saw a plane land out here."

"That old codger was a full bird colonel in Korea. He may be a drunk now, but he knows his aircraft and he described this one to a T," O'Neal answered. "The only place to hide a plane out here is that warehouse he told us about."

"As drunk as the old fella was I'm surprised he wasn't seeing pink elephants flying around on tiny wings." Wilbur shook his head. "I'd feel better with a squad behind me."

"I'm sure you would." A gruff female voice sounded from the darkness.

Wilbur turned to face a *C-96 Mauser* aimed at his head. He glanced up into the demented face of Baroness Blood. "Stupid American's."

O'Neal wheeled. His finger circled the trigger. "The Baroness." The .45 bucked in his hand.

"And she's not alone." Maxi-Mize's gigantic fist slammed the agents jaw, sending him reeling to the ground. He managed one last desperate squeeze of the trigger before darkness claimed him.

Wilbur turned to run, the taloned hand of The Vulture's Claw fastened on his head. A mind-numbing spasm shot through the Lieutenant's body. His eyes rolled back in the sockets, white drool came from his mouth, as he sank to his knees.

"This one works for Jack Munroe." Tina returned to her normal height and kicked the prone agent ribs. "They know we're here. Ghost Boy sent them."

"I don't think so." The Baroness shook her head. "If he knew where we are, he'd be here himself, with a lot more men. I think these two were searching and lucked onto this warehouse."

"Well, what are we going to do with them?" Tina asked.

"I think that's obvious." Von Tug's voice grated. "We have to kill them."

The Baroness smiled. "I haven't killed an American in years." She ran her hands over her thighs in ecstasy. "It's an experience I've longed to repeat."

"Let me do it," Tina said. "One quick shot to the back of their heads and it's finished."

"That's too easy, Child." The Baroness's cupped her left breast. "I want them conscious. I want them to feel their lives slipping away and beg for mercy as they die."

"Baroness, put aside your petty tortures for the moment." Tina stepped between her and the helpless men. "We don't have the time for this."

"Stand aside, Little Girl." Von Tug pulled her away. "Let the Baroness have her fun."

Gunfire erupted from the darkness, sparks flew from the crumpled concrete. The Baroness and Von Tug raced toward the open overhead doors. "There are more of them," she shouted. "We have to get out of here."

"Where is the girl?" Von Tug glanced over his shoulder.

Blood leaked from Tina's right shoulder and trickled down her arm dripping to the dry gritty earth. She pushed herself to her knees staring into the darkness.

"Get up," The Baroness shouted. "We must escape."

The young woman clamped her hand over the wound and crawled to a defensible position.

A burst of red fire came from the shooters position. Two bullets struck the hard concrete at Von Tug's feet. The Baroness disappeared, into the gloomy warehouse. Within seconds, the coughing belch of an aircraft engine filled the night air.

"Don't leave me." Tina jumped to her feet, and raced toward the gaping door. Bullets whizzed past her head. The breeze from the projectiles ruffled her hair.

The aircraft eased through the space. Tina saw the handles leading to the small passenger area.

"Hurry, Girl." Von Tug's deformed hand reached out for her her as the plane eased past.

Tina caught the bird-like appendage as the plane began to gather speed necessary for take-off. "Help me!" she screamed. "Help me, inside."

Two bullets struck the fuselage. Tina ducked her head instinctively. "Hurry, damn it."

Von Tug lifted her from the ground. "Come, Little One. We will have need of your powers when we get to Nevada." The veins stood out in his arms, as deposited her inside. "Did you see who was shooting at us?"

"Nein," she answered. "All I saw was muzzle flash."

"I wonder how they found us." Von Tug shook his head.

A set of high heels stepped into a shaft of moonlight. "Find the Mize girl's blood trail and drop this." Illyria's voice broke the silence. "Make it appear she dropped this when she fled."

"Do you think this is wise?" Kantorovich snapped the papers from her hand and hastened to do her bidding. "The American's aren't stupid, they'll be suspicious."

"Of course." Illyria tilted her head; a girlish giggle came from her lips. "I want the SOS waiting for them when they attack. It's vital the German's fail in their attempt. Ghost Boy will not expect two attacks on the base at the same time."

He moved to her side. "What of these two?"

"Let them live for now." An evil smile split her face. "We'll kill them later."

"Jack, I'm starving." Gloria squeezed the general's arm. "The Golden Horn is still open. We had some good times there."

"I should hang around the base in case Alex needs to contact me." Jack smiled. "But I'll treat you to the best meal in the mess hall."

Gloria rolled her eyes. "Alex will be the director of the SOS, one day. You need to give him some room. He'll do fine. He was trained by the best." She glanced up at the stars.

"Jack, someone's keeping tabs on us. On the sloped roof ahead, someone moved." Clutching his arm tighter, she steered him away from the wall. "I hope it's not your old girlfriend with the chalky skin and the red eyes." Her hand closed around the checkered grip of the .32 in her coat pocket.

"They're pink," Jack answered. "I can't get to my weapon."

"I've got this." Gloria moved closer. "If it's Bunny, I'll rip her white hair out."

"She's in France by now. She's not going to get caught up in this mess." He glanced at Gloria's face. "Where is he?"

"Twenty feet ahead, dark spot. He'll jump us there." Her grip on his arm eased. "Get ready."

"How in the hell did he get on base?" Jack mumbled.

"Maybe, he has hypnotic eyes, like Bunny." Gloria moved her hand to Jack's back, palm flat between his shoulder blades.

"Quit harping about her." Jack's spine tingled, as they entered into the circle of darkness.

Gloria shoved him forward. Jack responded immediately, his old training served him well as he rolled forward. He felt the sharp edge of a knife blade tugging at his shoulder, slicing into the thick material of his coat.

"No, you don't," Gloria shouted. A heavy body struck the side of the building.

Jack peered through the gloom. Two sets of legs moved through the inky blackness. He recognized Gloria's shapely limbs and kicked out at the attacker's thicker legs. A loud grunt rewarded his efforts.

"Get out of here, Jack." Gloria shouted. "I can handle it."

A low moan came from Gloria's lips, a crushing blow landed in her stomach. The pistol dropped from her fingers and clattered on the ground. Moonlight glinted from the knife in the killer's hand as he turned his attention to Jack.

Gloria rolled to a kneeling position. She kicked the attacker's leg. Her high heel impaled the soft flesh of his calf.

"Damn it." The attacker's right leg buckled. Jack recognized the face as he braced himself against the wall.

"Rogats, Erik Rogats." He lashed out, focusing his strength in one savage kick. His hard leather heel smashed the assassin's jaw. He melted to the ground with a solid thud.

Jack climbed to his feet and brushed dirt from his clothes. "Gloria, are you alright?"

No answer.

"Ranger Girl, Gloria, answer me?" Jack moved to the downed man's shoe, tugging the shoestring free, and bound the killer's thumbs together. "That'll hold him for a while." His eyes settled on Gloria, leaning against the wall.

"Damn it, why didn't you answer me?" He moved closer.

"Get a medic, Jack," she croaked. "He scratched me with that dagger, the tip's poisoned." She pressed her back to the building and slid to the ground. "He cut through my dress and bra, blade grazed my shoulder. I'm showing too much skin. Give me your coat before you call the MP's. I don't want anyone to see me like this."

Jack removed his jacket and draped it over her shoulders. The chill of the evening immediately cut through his shirt. "You'll be okay, Gloria," he mumbled. "I won't let anything happen to you."

He reached inside his pants pocket for his whistle. He'd carried it since basic training. He raised it to his lips. A loud shrill sound filled the night. "Guard! Guard!" he shouted. "We need help over here. Get a medic here now."

"Okay, guys, on your feet." Alex banged on the thin doors of Hideous and Lee Allyn sleeping quarters. "Got a message from O'Neal and Wilbur, they had a run in with Baroness Blood and Maxi-Mize last night. Get dressed. I want us in the air in thirty minutes."

"My God." Lee's disembodied voice mumbled. "It's still dark outside."

"Come on, get moving." Alex glanced at the guard assigned to the hallway. "Go get some sack time." He yanked open the door.

Hideous jumped to his feet. "Ready."

Alex glanced at the undisturbed bed. "Did you sleep on the floor?"

The man monster nodded.

"Hit the showers and change your clothes. We're going to Nevada. We'll be in a confined space for a few hours. We should all be at our best." Alex nodded. "I'll have POPS find you some clothes."

"Hideous not have bath or clean clothes in long time."

"I should have taken care of that detail last night, I apologize."

"Hey, Kid, how do O'Neal and the LT know where these Nazi creeps are going to attack?" Lee stumbled through the door, tugging his shirt on his invisible frame.

"They had a dust-up with them last night. They knocked them out and fled. During a search of the property O'Neal found a map. Tina was hit during the gunfire, so she may not be a factor in this battle." Alex turned to leave. "We're going to the Nevada Proving Ground."

"Doesn't that seem very convenient?" Lee snapped awake. "That's a plant and you know it."

"They are performing a nuclear test on the fourth. Now get dressed. Hideous is in the shower. Things might smell better in the plane if he bathed and changed out of those rags." Alex turned down the hallway.

"We're walking into a trap." Lee scratched his head.

Deep furrows wrinkled Alex's forehead. "I've thought about that. We'll take every precaution." He glanced at the shirt that appeared to be floating in the air. "Do you always sleep in the nude?"

Lee paused for a moment. "Most of the time, with my unique affliction it's better. My wife never got used to it." He tugged on his trousers. "Do you have another of these crazy pistols?"

"I'll have extras loaded on the plane." A smile crinkled his face. "Get some chow. We leave as soon as Hideous is ready."

"I was hoping you'd leave him here." Lee shook his head.

"I've got to keep an eye on him." Alex shrugged. "So he goes."

The pickup struck a huge chug-hole, pitching the passengers forward. Von Tug down-geared as the vehicle moved slowly over the rub-board trail.

"The slug went through, didn't hit any bones." The Baroness tugged the blood crusted bandage from Tina's shoulder.

Tina winced as the bandage stuck to the wound, a string of blood threaded to her elbow. "How much longer do we have to ride in this heap?" she asked through gritted teeth.

"The rendezvous point should be nearby." Baroness Blood answered. "I was a nurse before the war. Flying was my one love, when the *Luftwaffe* discovered my talents they gave me a plane, forty-five confirmed kills." A prideful smile beamed from her face.

"Quit talking." Tears leaked from the corners of Tina's closed eyes. "The Americans will be expecting us."

"I have a bad feeling about this mission, and I don't think Tina's up to a fight." Von Tug glanced toward the Baroness. "We may have to do this one on our own."

"And split her share of the money between us." She ran a hand through her long blonde locks. A malicious glint twinkled in her eyes.

"You're not leaving me behind. I'm going on this operation." Tina's eyes opened to bare slits. "You can have my share. I don't care about the money. I want to free my sister."

"That's very generous of you, *Klein-madchen.*" The Baroness pulled sulfa powder from the first aid kit and filled the wound. "After we have the money, I will help you."

"As will I." Von Tug growled. "I don't trust Illyria, and that fancy Russian. I'd like to sink my talons into his neck and rip out his throat."

"Worry about him later," the Baroness scolded. She wrapped fresh bandages around the wound and applied a generous application of medical tape. "We'll kill Kantorovich after this is finished."

Von Tug flashed his teeth in a wide grin. "I'll enjoy watching him die."

The worn brakes of the truck screeched as it came to a stop. "We're here." Von Tug climbed from the antique rig. He stood in the center of the road, gazing off into the distance. "It's hotter than the gates of Hades out here."

"Where are Illyria and her dog?" The Baroness jumped to the ground. "They were supposed to meet us here with supplies."

"Help me with the girl," Von Tug barked. "Perhaps we could locate the base on our own?"

"We don't know the location of our target," she answered. "We will wait; the rest will do Tina good."

Tina swung her legs to the ground, her injured arm cradled to her chest. She licked her lips and staggered to the rear of the pickup. Her pasty white face wrinkled in agony.

"You should stay here; we'll come for you when we're finished." Loose dust puffed from Von Tug's boots. "You can barely walk."

"I can make it." Tina shrugged his helping hand away. "I have Illyria's word. She will help me free Cheryl. She will keep her promise to me."

"Here." The baroness grabbed her hand. "Move to the far side of the pickup, out of the sun. That'll give you some relief."

"I can walk on my own." Tina grimaced, each stride jarring her shoulder. She collapsed to her knees and crawled around the vehicle. "How much water do we have?"

"Only a couple of swallows." The baroness shook the canteen. She turned to Von Tug. "If we could find the base would we be able to fight?"

"I can." He nodded. "I believe Tina could if she weren't inured, but in these conditions, I don't believe either of you could make it."

"Someone is coming." Tina raised herself to her knees, staring down along the dirt road. "It may be Illyria."

The Baroness gazed at the billowing dust cloud. "Too many things have gone wrong with this operation. I'm thinking we should pull out."

"I can't wait." Tina forced her wobbly legs to bear her weight. "This is the best opportunity I've had to free Cheryl." She leaned against the pickup.

The Baroness's fisted hands settled on her shapely hips. "I have doubts about Illyria's intentions."

" YOU'RE NOT LEAVING ME BEHIND. "

A *Jeep* appeared ahead of the massive dust plume. The driver slid to a stop beside the haggard trio.

"We don't have much time," Illyria shouted. Dust covered her Khaki shirt and Jodhpurs; she wiped the settling powder from her face, and jumped to the ground. "Take the supplies and go. Here is a map; the base is twenty miles north. When the American forces moves to deal with your incursion, Kantorovich and I will creep into the base and steal the weapon."

"Illyria, we need to talk, I don't like this, to many things have gone wrong." The Baroness stepped toward the *Jeep*.

"Now is not the time. If we are to succeed you must go now." Her intense gaze settled on the blonde. "If you're losing your courage, Baroness, I understand. This assignment has been very taxing."

"Get in." Von Tug grabbed the blonde's shoulder, and helped Tina to her feet. "We've got a job to do."

"You have food, water and weapons." Illyria's hand settled on the pistol grip at her waist. She turned as Tina struggled into the *Jeep*. "What happened to her?"

"We were attacked in New Mexico. Tina was shot." The Baroness leaned against the vehicle's hot metal frame. "Don't play me for a fool, Illyria. If this is a ploy to sacrifice us for your own agenda, you will regret that decision." The corners of her mouth lifted in an evil smile.

"You're wasting time." Illyria's hate-filled eyes returned the intense glare. "You must leave now, if we are to succeed."

"Remember, what I said." Von Tug popped the clutch, the wheels spun in the gravel. The *Jeep* left the road and bumped over the uneven ground.

Jack sat in the uncomfortable chair, and held Gloria's hand. He glanced at the IV drip feeding medication into her bloodstream. The medics and the MP's had arrived in time. An old sawbones injected her with anti-venom, and saved her life.

"General." A young sergeant stuck his head in the door. "Todd Matthews, Sir, I'm in charge of the guard detail assigned to the hospital."

Jack turned a weary eye toward the non-com. "Take good care of her. She's very important."

"It's morning, Sir." Matthews licked his lips nervously. "Shouldn't you return to base and dress for the funeral?"

He nodded. "Yeah, I need to get going." He climbed to his feet, patting Gloria's cheek one last time. "I don't want anyone, but doctors and nurses in this room. Do you understand me?" Jack growled.

"Yes, Sir." The Sergeant snapped to attention. "Any other instructions, Sir?"

Jack shook his head. "After the funeral, I want to have a chat with Rogats. Pass the word to your superiors, and have him ready when I return."

Matthews swallowed hard lump in his throat. "Yes, Sir."

Jack left the room and made his way down the stairs, then crossed the parade ground to his quarters. He had just enough time for breakfast and a quick shower before he changed for the services. A black staff car waited in front of his temporary quarters.

"Good morning, Sir." The sergeant snapped to attention. "You're cutting it close, Sir."

Jack nodded. "I'll be ready in a half-hour."

An hour later he stood at the back of the huge crowd. Jack followed a short squatty dignitary toward the open casket. The former Prime Minister was dressed in his finest suit, age and illness had weakened the firm set of his jaw. Jack paused at the coffin, glancing at the man who rallied Britain during those terrible years when Hitler and the Nazis threatened the world.

A hand descended on his shoulder. "Time to move on soldier, the old bulldog's at rest now."

He turned to face General Omar Bradley. "You're right, Brad." Jack nodded. "He's done his duty." He resumed his place in the procession and passed through a side door into the bright sunshine, General Bradley followed.

"How are things, Jack?" General Bradley removed his spectacles, cleaning the lenses.

"They're good, Brad. How are you?"

"I've heard good things about the SOS." The general returned the glasses to his nose. "Lyndon thinks very highly of your organization. My people tell me you have Erik Rogats in the brig."

Jack's mouth dropped open in surprise. "How did you find out?"

"That's not important. Things are heating up back in the states." General Bradley nodded. "I'll take care of things here, I've got some boys lined up to question Rogats, and I'll see to it that Gloria is taken care of. You need to get back home and deal with the situation there."

"Thanks, Brad." Jack grasped the general's hand and gave it a firm shake. "But Alex can handle things."

General Bradley shook his head. "I think he's still a little green."

"No, Brad. The kid will do fine."

⋮ ⋮ ⋮

"Where are they?" Lee Allyn whispered into the wrist communicator. He wiped sweat from his brow and exhaled a deep breath.

"They're here. I picked up Tina's thought patterns before she activated the scrambler." Ghost Boy flew high circles above the perimeter fence, maintaining his invisibility and flying were beginning to take a toll on his energy. "They'll attack soon."

"I feel like a sitting duck out here." Lee glanced toward Hideous. "Stand up straight, you're supposed to be a soldier, and keep your back to the fence. If they see that snout of yours, they'll know it's a trap."

The man monster shrugged. "Not like uniform, itches."

"They're coming toward you. Wait until they're inside, if you move too quick we'll come up with an empty sack." Ghost Boy whispered.

"They come, Hideous smell them. One hurt, smell blood."

Small arms fire struck the *Jeep* with a metallic ping. Baroness Blood charged from concealment, firing a *C-96 Mauser*. Lee and Hideous dropped to the ground.

Tina appeared to the left, jogging toward the fence, her arm cradled at her waist. She grew to her full height of twenty feet. Von Tug ran by her side. She lifted the German, he curled into a ball, as her arm shot forward. He did a forward roll in midair and landed on his feet near the *Jeep*.

"Alright, let's take 'em." Ghost Boy descended from the heavens, turning visible. He fired his pulse gun at the Baroness.

"Come on, let's go." Lee's knuckles whitened around the grip of the large pistol.

"Me ready. Not have good fight in many years." The elongated jaw split into a grin. "Not since I fight you."

"Well you're going to have one now." Lee rolled from the protection of the vehicle, firing the electronic weapon at Tina. "Everybody is inside, pick your target."

The blast went wide of the mark and struck the fence. Tina whirled and triggered two quick shots at the pair, kicking up dirt and grit at Lee's feet.

Hideous bounded high in the air, his prodigious leaps carried him toward the Vulture's Claw. His fist slammed the Nazi's jaw. A smile twisted Von Tug's bloodied lips.

"You'll have to do better than that." He drove the clawed hand forward. Sharp talons pierced the man-monster's thick hide. A scream of agony burst from wolf-like lips as he struggled to escape the German's grip.

Hideous gritted his teeth, hands closed on Von tug's wrists. His large feet left the ground and settled in the German's belly. The uneven weight distribution forced Von Tug forward. The creature's back struck the ground, corded muscles bunched in his powerful legs propelling the Nazi high in the air.

The breath burst from the German's lungs on impact. He struggled to his feet. Electricity surged through his body. He grew rigid, chin pointed toward the heavens, teeth gritted together. He crossed his arms in front of his chest. "Vhat iss this?" he shouted, the words unintelligible.

The German turned toward the source of his torment. "Captain Zero," he mumbled, making eye contact with the former OSS agent. "I vill kill you for this." Fighting back the pain, he took an agonizing step forward.

"Yeah, it's me." Lee gave the power dial a twist; the gauge went into the danger zone. "You're not getting away this time."

Von Tug twisted at an unnatural angle, unable to move. He slowly sank to his knees. A line of drool ran from his mouth, as he collapsed, unconscious.

"Leave him alone." Tina's massive left hand slammed Captain Zero's face. Lee flew through the air, landed roughly on his shoulders and rolled through the gritty soil.

"Get the other one," The Baroness screamed. "Hurry, kill him." A blast from Ghost Boy's pulse gun blasted a hole in the ground at her feet. She dove for cover behind the abandoned *Jeep*.

Tina swung a mighty blow at Hideous. The man-monster dodged the attempt and leaped at the woman's injured shoulder. The Baroness met him in mid leap; her extra weight forced him to the ground.

*Where are Kantorovich and Illyria?* Ghost Boy scanned the parched Nevada desert. *They have to be close.* He studied the ground below, searching for any sign of the pair.

"POPS, any sign of Illyria or Kantorovich at the base?" He spoke into the wrist communicator.

"Everything is quiet here." POPS answered. "The base is on high alert, everyone is armed and ready."

"Hey, Kid," Lee shouted. "We need a little help over here."

Maxi-Mize pinned Hideous to the ground with her left arm. The Baroness pounded on his skull with the *Mauser.*

Captain Zero forced himself to his knees. Blood ran down from a huge gash on his forehead. His arm quivered as he lifted the pulse gun to shoulder level.

Alex glided above Tina. The pulse gun bucked in his hand. The effect was immediate. Tina arched her back, twitching in agony. Violent spasms tore the bandage from her arm. Fresh blood threaded to her elbow and dripped to the ground. A scream of anguish ripped from her lips.

Lee fired at the Baroness. The weak charge in his pistol knocked her from the man monster but did little damage. She jumped to her feet and bolted toward the fence. Alex fired a short burst that caught her in mid-stride. She collapsed and slid face first across the pebbly surface.

Tina dwindled to her normal height. She fell to her back, pawing the air. "Cheryl, is Cheryl okay?"

"She's fine. You'll see her soon." Alex landed near Lee and helped the former OSS agent to his feet. "POPS, we've got them."

"Lee, you and Hideous handle things here." He leaped into the air. "We've got to find Illyria and Kantorovich."

∴ ∴ ∴

A loud explosion sent shock waves through the air. The *Jeep* flipped in the air, landing on the roof. A fierce wind buffeted Alex. He tumbled through the air, out of control, the hot sand rushed to meet him.

"I think they found us," Lee shouted. "Where are they?"

Alex concentrated, his mental probes sweeping the surrounding area. Two mental signatures appeared in his mind, Illyria and Kantorovich.

*Prepare to die, Ghost Boy.* Illyria's hate-filled thoughts burst in his brain. *You can't escape.*

Alex crawled to Lee's side, far behind the burning *Jeep.* He glanced to the side, Hideous and the German's lay scattered from the force of the blast.

"What the hell are they shooting at us?" Lee moved away from the flames.

"A modified Dragunov, with exploding bullets." Alex brushed sand from his forehead. "I'll be back in a minute." He slapped Lee on the shoulder.

"What are you going to do?" Lee demanded.

"I'm going to turn intangible and try to find their position," Alex concentrated, his body faded but remained visible, like a sun faded photograph.

*I'm sure you've tried to turn invisible by now.* Illyria's taunting thoughts burned in his mind. *We're coated in a fine dust that interferes with your mental power. Come out now, and we'll spare your companions.*

"What's going on?" Lee demanded.

"Illyria's gloating. She said if I surrender, she'll spare the rest of you."

"She's lying." Lee eased his head to the side of the wreckage, peering at the wide open space. "I wish we had a good long range weapon. Even if I saw them I doubt these pulse guns could do any damage at this range."

A second bullet struck the sand below the *Jeep*. The deafening explosion threw the crumpled hunk of metal high into the air. Flaming bits of wreckage rained down on Alex and Lee.

*You don't have much time.* Illyria laughed. *The next one goes into your hairy friend and the German's.*

Hideous rolled into a small depression, his hand circled the *C-96 Mauser.* His sensitive nose caught the scent of the intruders. He crawled forward slowly, moving over the scorching sand. "Hideous not like evil man."

A glint of metal caught Ghost Boy's eye. It disappeared briefly behind a thin layer of clouds. *That's POPS, it has to be.* "POPS, get out of here." He shouted into the wrist communicator. "Illyria has a special rifle, it fires exploding bullets."

*Your communicator isn't working.* Illyria teased. "Ivan, take down the robot."

Ghost Boy grabbed the pulse gun, firing ahead of the flying robot. The blast singed the air ahead of the mechanical man, POPS changed course. The air quivered with concussive force, the exploding bullet struck a metal foot. The blast knocked POPS into an awkward spiral. The robot crashed to the ground.

POPS ravaged body lay in a heap. His leg reduced to jagged bits of crumpled metal. "Alex, what is happening?" Metal fingers pawed the loose sand, the mechanical man tried in vain to pull his massive body from harm's way.

*They played me like an idiot.* Alex leaped into the air, his flight slow and erratic. *Illyria wanted me to know about the Nazi's. This was an elaborate trap.*

Ghost Boy dove toward the ground, a fierce wind buffeted his head as the bullet whirled past. He leaped into the air, flying straight toward the sun, betting his life on a desperate gamble.

His strength slowly returned, the faint wind plucked the tiny bits of dust from his clothes and person.

∶ ∶ ∶

"Kill him, you idiot." Illyria's hand fisted in his collar. "Kill him."

Kantorovich wiped tears from his eyes. "His back is to the sun, I can't find him."

"Find him and kill him."

∶ ∶ ∶

*Alex, I'm close. I can smell them.* The bizarre thoughts of the man beast jolted his mind. *Be ready.* Ghost Boy located Illyria and Kantorovich, he folded his arms to his body and aimed himself at the pair. Sun reflected from the telescope as the Russian sniper tried to locate him.

The Queen of Spies held her hands over the glass to break the blinding glare of the sun. Kantorovich waved her away, climbing to his feet, he pressed the rifle to his cheek, his finger tightened on the trigger.

Hideous leaped to his feet, his large fingers pressed into the trigger guard. A loud animal scream burst from his throat as he raced toward the pair squeezing the trigger rapidly.

"Damn you, you filthy beast." Illyria shouted, she yanked the pistol from her shoulder holster, with calm deliberation she fired.

Hideous stumbled, but refused to fall, he continued to rain bullets at the pair. A red rose blossomed on Kantorovich's shirt front. The Russian sank to his knees, his weak hands wrapped around the wooden stock.

"Illyria, help me." He screamed.

The Queen of Spies, cast her eyes toward the onrushing Ghost Boy and shifted to the wounded creature approaching from the side. "Not today, Comrade." She holstered the pistol and ran to the waiting *Jeep.*

The engine caught easily, Lady Illyria disappeared in a cloud of dust. Ghost Boy slowed his headlong dive and slowly descended to the ground, staring at the wounded assassin.

"Alex Conroy." Kantorovich smiled. "We meet at last."

Ghost Boy placed his foot on the Russian's chest and pushed him to the ground. "If anyone on my team dies, you'll stand before the firing squad."

Kantorovich's eyes narrowed to slits.

"Your Soviet bosses have a lot to answer for." Alex eased his foot from the Russians chest.

"The Russian Government did not send us here. Lady Illyria and I defected over a month ago. We lied to the Nazi's to enlist their aid. Our employer wanted you dead." Kantorovich struggled to a sitting position. "You were blinded by the threat of the Nazi's and did not see our real mission."

"You're lying." Alex scanned the Russian's mind. His probes blunted by the image of a solid brick wall.

A lop-sided grin crossed his face. "We will still win."

"Jack's going to love talking with you." Ghost Boy grabbed Kantorovich by the collar and pulled the assassin to his feet. "I hope you enjoy prison."

Jack Munroe stood on the tarmac beaming, as the DC-9 struck the surface and gradually came to a stop. The huge cargo doors opened, Alex Conroy walked down the ramp beside Hideous, stained bandages covered the man monster's chest, Lee Allyn walked slowly behind him.

"You did great, Kid." Jack pulled a cigar from his pocket and peeled the cellophane away.

"How can you say that?" Alex shook his head. "Illyria got away, Hideous and Lee are wounded and POPS' leg is ruined."

"She hasn't made it out of the country yet. I've got O'Neal and Wilbur working on her location." He fished a lighter from his pocket and puffed the stogie to life. "You guys look a little worse for wear. I'll expect detailed reports by morning."

"Yes Sir." Alex nodded. "I'd like to get started on POPS new leg as soon as possible."

Jack shook his head. "I've got some of the brains coming in to give POPS an overall. I need you in Texas, O'Neal and Wilbur will be expecting you. We have to stop Illyria."

A huge, heavy-duty lift moved forward to transport the robot to the lab.

"You would've been proud of him, Jack." Lee slapped Alex on the back. "For his first time in command he did fine."

"Get in that truck. You're both going to the base hospital." A wreath of smoke circled Jacks face. "The commander at Area 51 has been calling ever since you dropped off the prisoners. He's not happy having so many criminals in his care. He wants us to send him some help."

Jack turned to Hideous and Captain Zero. "You clowns have a job if you want it. The president has authorized me to hire you to oversee security at Area 51."

"What are you saying?" Lee paused, one foot poised on the truck rail.

"Hideous needs someone to keep tabs on him, and you need a job." Jack smiled. "Besides, Lyndon likes the way you guys work together. Report in after you visit with your family. Now you need to heal up."

Lee settled into the truck, smiled, and nodded to the general as it pulled away.

"You did a good thing for those two." Alex settled onto the passenger seat.

"We can't let Hideous run around without supervision." Jack climbed behind the wheel of the waiting *Jeep*. "He ran with a rough crowd back in the thirties, they made him into an attack dog. Lyndon's giving him a break. He's on a work release program."

"We've got to find Illyria." Alex let a deep breath hiss from his lips.

"We'll get her." Jack turned the key. The engine coughed and sputtered to life. "Get a good night's rest, you're back on the case tomorrow."

## *THE END*

# WRITING GHOST BOY

It's a privilege to write a Ghost Boy adventure. I mean what's not to like about Alex Conroy. He has a grumpy general, as his boss and mentor and a robot for a sidekick. His adventures take him to some out of the way places and he encounters some of the worst bad guys imaginable.

During the sixties, spies were well represented in movies, on television, in dozens of paperbacks and in comics. I remember watching the creations of Ian Fleming and Donald Hamilton at the movies and reading their adventures in paperback. Matt Helm was always one of my favorites. I picked up Death of a Citizen in a used book store and instantly became a fan. I've read nearly every Matt Helm novel ever produced. James Bond also had a special place on my bookshelf, but I also found other characters, such as Sam Durrell and Nick Carter, Killmaster.

I loved the televised adventures of The Man from U.N.C.L.E., I-Spy, The Avengers and Secret Agent Man. One of the local stores in town had comics; through this medium I discovered Tower Comics T.H.U.N.D.E.R. Agents and Harvey Comics short-lived Spyman.

Alex Conroy could walk side by side with these characters. I can see him fighting side by side with Napoleon Solo and Illya Kuryakin against the evil minions of T.H.R.U.S.H., and assisting Kelly Robinson and Alexander Scott on an undercover assignment in South America. He would do battle against the forces of darkness with Noman and Dynamo and stalk the back alleys of Paris with James Bond or the Arizona desert with Matt Helm.

Ghost Boy is that kind of hero. His adventures take him to small out of the way places and into crowded cities. He's the kind of guy everyone would like to have on their side. Hopefully I be able to chronicle his adventures for a long time.

**TERRY ALEXANDER** - and his wife Phyllis live on a small farm in East Central Oklahoma. They have three children and nine Grandchildren. Terry is a member of The Fictioneers, Oklahoma Writers Federation, Ozark Creative Writers and the Arkansas Ridge Writers. He has been published in various anthologies from Knightwatch Press, Pulp Empire, Pro Se Press, Moonstone Books, Wicked East Press and AirShip 27.

# RISE OF THE
# ATOMIC ARMY
## J. WALT LAYNE

June 1964

Alex Conroy a young man of about twenty, tall, blond, military fit and uncomfortable in his tuxedo sat at a finely appointed table complete with a crisp linen tablecloth. He was running calculations on three slide rules and scribbling madly on a linen napkin with a fountain pen. A shadow passed behind him, but he didn't look up. The owner of the shadow tried to read the equation algorithm in the reflection of the crystal water glass to no success.

Both Alex and his not so casual observer appeared oblivious to the White House State Dinner happening around them, neither of them were what they appeared. Along with processing a very complex proof of matter in material space, Alex was monitoring the communications of the Secret Service Agents, and using POPS (Photoelectric Optimal Protection Sentry) to analyze a number of radio-static anomalies that he was feeling peripheral to his heightened perception.

As the passerby moved to an adjacent table Alex continued his calculations, sometimes with a slide rule in each hand. His outward persistence and appearance of being lost in thought was anything but. He was casually eavesdropping on a dozen conversations all pertaining to different facets of the same subject matter- The impression of a state dinner on a nation grieving the loss of its president and popular culture icon, the rise of communism everywhere, and the war in Vietnam.

Just then a hand rested on his shoulder and gave it a sound squeeze. Alex knew the owner of the hand before he heard the voice say, "Alex, you are always working. Does your mind never leave the lab?" Alex lowered his pen and started to get up, but the hand on his shoulder was firm. "No Son, don't get up. If it's all the same Petra and I will join you until the receiving line begins, and then we have to go to the head table."

Alex smiled, "Great, I'm almost finished."

"What is that, exactly?" Garman Fitch, Director of CIA asked as he

**51**

pulled out a chair for his wife, Petra. She sat as he pushed the chair in beneath her. After slight adjustment Fitch sank into the chair next to Alex and the man feared by presidents, subordinates and peers, spoke with Alex Conroy as if they were school chums.

Alex smiled and looked at the linen napkin, then did a double take. He tapped the pen cap on the initial equation, the formula which he'd scribbled to the side, and then on each subset. Then back to the formula, added a jot or tittle, here and there and then drew his signature doubled underline beneath the proof, "Holy smokes!"

Fitch's face fractured into what would have to pass for a smile, "What is it?"

Alex turned the napkin slightly and Garman stared at what may as well have been a cuneiform translation of The Gettysburg Address. "Chicken tracks to me son. Anything more complicated than the checkbook and I delegate to the secretary of my treasury," he shot Petra a sidelong glance. She smiled at him and adjusted her shawl.

"This is a proof I wanted to show Dr. Einstein, but I don't see him." Alex said, distracted.

"No, he usually avoids these things," Fitch looked around as the band played *As the Cason Goes Rolling Along.* "Bully on him, I'd rather be home myself." Fitch scanned the room, "Proof of what?"

Alex picked up on something, a vague pulsing, and almost inaudible but creating sound pressure. He tried to raise POPS telepathically as he answered, "On matters pertaining to matter, space is relative to matter."

Fitch's lack of understanding wasn't as alarming as POPS failure to respond. Granted radio communications were sometimes difficult due to layers of building materials, but never had there been an issue with telepathic communication. The band struck up *Hail to the Chief* and Fitch and his wife dissolved into a gathering crowd. Alex tried to raise POPS again as he watched Tim Torrez, the White House Press Secretary take the dais and walk to the podium.

"Blockade, lockdown. Stagehands to curtain, Alamo is moving." Alex heard the communication from the Secret Service OIC to his team chiefs. On the dais, the Marine honor guard snapped to attention and executed their movements as the band played a second chorus of *Hail to the Chief.* Alex knew what most of the guests did not, while all eyes were on the honor guard all exits and entrances were closed and secured by armed agents. The door from which the president supposedly entered from led to a blind hallway where a platoon of armed men waited at the ready to defend the president, who waited in a secure bullet and bombproof room, also under guard, behind the curtained entryway.

The President moved to the platform within a phalanx of Secret Service Agents and a hush fell on the room, as Lyndon Johnson ascended the steps. This was the first event since the assassination of President Kennedy nearly a year before. Many journalists stated that this event was inappropriate considering the state of national mourning, but the decision was made to save the date due to the growing concern over the escalating war in Vietnam and mounting number of casualties.

As Johnson walked toward the podium Alex sensed movement in his periphery and turned his head. The man who had earlier peered over his shoulder had left his chair and was storming the dais. As security personnel leapt into action to intercept him an ultrasonic weapon of some type began to buffet at a crippling frequency from all corners of the room. As military and secret servicemen began to crumple the man continued toward the dais.

"POPS, I need you, countermeasures. Locate the signal's source and jam it." Alex said into a wrist communicator, trying this secondary means of communication as he left his seat, tearing after the man.

Alex crossed the dance floor, but as he closed on the man, some unseen force prevented him from getting any closer. Alex redoubled his effort, but it was as if a manifold of space had opened between him and the man who, though not in a particular hurry, continued toward the President at an alarmingly unabated rate.

Behind him, Alex heard General Jack Munroe calling for the man to halt. Alex suddenly changed direction and felt himself move along the axis of the manifold. Somehow a secret service agent drew his Colt 1911 and fired a shot.

Alex watched as the man turned and drew a futuristic looking pistol. He tried again to summon POPS to no avail. He focused his mind on the large bass drum couched on its stand near the brass band. Though it was within the manifold he was able to raise it and hurl it toward the gunman. The air around the man crackled with radio static energy when the drum impacted, sending him to his knees.

"Didn't see that coming did you?" Alex thought and turned his focus to a pair of chairs.

Suddenly the bullet penetrated the manifold and the man vanished as it closed. The round itself was stretched, elongated into a six inch long copper jacketed dart, which pinned something to the head of the bald eagle on The Seal of the President of the United States which was affixed to the front of the podium.

It all happened so fast. The vacuum caused by the closing manifold sucked Alex off his feet. His mass and inertia released all potential energy along the kinetic path he'd been on before the change of direction which had allowed him to move along the manifold in place of moving through it. He crashed headlong into the front of the platform.

"What in the hell was that?" Jack Munroe asked as he pulled Alex to his feet.

"The President!" Alex turned with a start to see Johnson trying to assess the situation from within the closed phalanx of Secret Servicemen.

"He's fine. Everybody's fine, except maybe that feller's gonna have a headache, when he gets to wherever he disappeared to." Munroe growled.

"Does anyone know that man? Do you have a copy of the guest list?" Alex asked, climbing the stairs onto the stage. He walked to the podium where the sheet of vellum hung from the dart. Alex fought the urge to cough as a cloud of putrid cigar smoke announced that Munroe had followed him.

"Well kid, what do you make of that?" Munroe asked as he pulled the vellum free.

Alex tore the vellum off the dart and tried to read the message written in a particularly maniacal bold scrawl. As he tipped it one way and another in the light the message seemed to self translate into as many languages as there were degrees of refraction, as if it based display on the photo temperature of the light. Orienting it finally to English it read:

*-You puny people. You petty, warlike, peddlers of death and despotic supplication. You will surrender yourselves or destruction shall follow-* *General Adama Neutronov, Commander of the Atomic Army.*

Alex looked at Munroe and was about to speak when the familiar voice of Phil Westrick, interrupted, "General, the President would like to speak with you." Munroe nodded and turned to go, leaving Alex puzzling over the piece of vellum. "You too, Alex. The old man asked for you first, but you know Munroe loves it when they need him."

Alex frowned, "I'd love to realize my father's dream of a world where warriors were a relic of the past, but we're not there yet. Jack Munroe and men like him may very well still have lessons to teach us."

Jack Munroe briefed the President and conferred with Alex for a more scientific explanation. The President considered this for a moment and surveyed the still recovering crowd including the joint chiefs and his most trusted advisors. "Jack I don't fully understand but you and that kid need to brief the Secretary of Defense and the Joint Chiefs at 0500." He looked directly at Alex, "In the mean time can you make all resources of S.O.S. available to NASA and the Air Force so maybe we can get a bead on whose party this was?"

"Yes Sir. We'll get right on it!"

An hour later Alex arrives at his lab in the Scientific Operational Security compound to find POPS in a state of electronic hibernation. Forethought for such a situation had caused Alex to add a process to POPS proprietary intelligence system to encrypt all data as the first step in the power cycle, thus turning him off nullifies efforts to tamper with his systems. A measure decided upon when communist spies were arrested on the campus of another defense technology contractor in town.

"So sorry Alex, but as I was running your calculations I was interrupted by a transmission attempting to jam our communication. Due to the nature of the ECM I thought it best to power down and not risk an attempt to access my superficial networks." The robot apologized.

"Good move. I doubt the world is ready for the technology which constitutes your make up." Alex smiled at the gleaming blue giant.

"I've always considered myself too progressive for my own good." POPS replied.

Alex sank onto a stool at the end of a large worktable. POPS came over and turned a massive roll of paper that hung on a heavy steel rack at the end of the table. When he'd pulled the quarter inch gridded paper the length of the table and fixed it in place the robot took his place across the table from Alex.

"We have a problem POPS." Alex began and explained what had happened at the White House.

"It would appear at face value that this person has found a way to manipulate space through some device. I posit that the device must be carried on his person and is only effective on objects traveling at subsonic speed in a small local area. The other issue, the sonic weapon you describe, also must be on his person, this weapon however has a much longer range and can be catastrophic."

"The President wants me to brief the Secretary of Defense and The Joint Chiefs at 0500. I need something to…" The uncontrollable urge to sneeze came over Alex as he searched his pockets for a handkerchief while trying to hold it in.

Not being a man accustomed to wearing a suit, his first reaction was to plunge a hand into his left hip pocket, which on his tuxedo trousers, happened to be sewn shut. Left front pocket yielded nothing but keys. He fished in the right pocket and thought he'd struck gold until he realized that instead of a handkerchief he was about to blow his nose on the linen napkin on which he'd written his relative space algorithm. Too late. The sneeze exploded as he turned away from the table in search of a paper towel.

"Alex, for what purpose was it necessary to desecrate a linen napkin with India ink?" POPS glib attempt at humor was followed immediately by a barrage of very wet sneezes.

"Great, I finally have a worthy problem and I'm getting a cold." Alex grumbled, blowing his nose and washing his hands with an anti-microbial soap of his own concoction.

When he returned to the table Alex spread open the napkin and oriented it so that POPS could read it into his logical and theoretical processing systems, which worked together much like a human brain to allow complex abstract intellectual calculations.

"In the given amount of time we cannot replicate the circumstances in order to understand how he's managed to open a manifold of space that he can manipulate relative to matter." POPS explained as his system began to extrapolate the data.

"No, but we can play to the hypothesis that the anomaly is generated by a device, and if that is the case, then the device must be carried on his person." Alex replied as an initial solution came to him, "Then you can design a smaller version of the communications jamming equipment we patented for Boeing to use in the Super Fortress."

"Brilliant idea, Alex," POPS rambled on as Alex transcribed his calculations from the napkin onto the large sheet of grid paper that POPS had affixed to the table.

Alex glanced up at the seven foot tall robot who was apparently awaiting his next instruction. "POPS, can you start prototyping an ECM which is not dependent on a present frequency?"

"Certainly, I was simply waiting for you to ask. It should not just be assumed that I should carry my end of the workload." POPS said very dryly.

"It must be time for your oil change and processor adjustment" Alex quipped.

"A derivation of our standard device should be a suitable place to begin." POPS said as he moved to another worktable.

Most of three hours later Alex was still working out a theoretical proof of his algorithm when he felt the floor vibrate beneath his feet. A moment later the vibration was followed by the sound of a hydraulic cylinder and the chuff of a micro compressor firing as POPS massive mechanical hand dropped a small apparatus on the table in front of him.

"Try this, Alex." POPS indicated a green button situated next to an unlit indicator lamp.

Alex lowered his pencil and grabbed the device without much thought. He turned it over in his hands and then pressed the button. The instant he did so, the indicator lamp went solid red and the room was assaulted by a debilitating sonic pitch. He punched the button again and the blaring noise ceased.

Alex shook his head and swallowed a couple of times in an attempt to clear his still ringing ears, "And which problem exactly was that supposed to address?"

"It was a test, Alex. This device operates within the known audio phonic spectrum between 100 hertz and at or below 10 Gigahertz. However the sonic weapon will most likely operate outside the device's range so I recommend ordinary low tech sound dampening to protect the hearing. There is little that can be done to dampen the sound energy's effect on the body. In either case the apparatus will provide a window of opportunity for a few seconds. Once he realizes that the weapon is having no effect, he will simply disappear again."

"Or worse," Alex exhaled slowly.

"Yes. One can safely assume that if this Neutronov is in possession of this technology as a defense mechanism, that his offensive technologies must be equally advanced."

"Thanks POPS now kill that racket so I can turn this thing off and try something."

The robot moved away momentarily and returned with a pair of heavily padded ear muffs, "I believe you'll want these in a moment."

Alex nodded, "When you're ready, let's test it without the device from super low range to ultra high."

Before the words were out of his mouth, Alex felt the uneasy discomfort of intense low frequency radiant sound pressure as it pulsed through him. As the sound intensity escalated his discomfort became the uneasiness associated with peristalsis followed quickly by weakness, confusion and nausea.

The effects changed as POPS progressed from low to high range.

Alex was physically struggling to make his hands obey him and put the headphones on as the shrill sound and ultrasonic pressure made his ears and eyes hurt. His teeth felt brittle. He was nearly in tears when the sound ceased.

After a moment of recovery Alex said, "Okay POPS, again." He switched on the small electronic countermeasure device and laid the headphones aside. "Troops won't have these, only plugs if they're lucky. Go ahead, give it all you got."

This time the low range sound was every bit as loud, but felt like distant thunder rumbling. As the pitch increased, however the rumbling dropped off and there was only the compressed remnants of the piercing sound with no physical effect.

Alex checked the device thinking that POPS had concluded the test. As he pressed the button he immediately felt a low range vibration that seemed to emanate from nowhere but was at once immobilizing. The bass range of the tone was beneath the range of the contraption and intensified to the point that Alex was being overcome by the urge to run. It became more of a presence than a sound. Alex gave POPS the cut sign and the force of the sound energy ceased. "We only have as long as it takes them to figure it out." Alex said as he again recovered from the physical effects of sound.

Alex looked across the conference table at the joint chiefs of the armed forces and tried to calculate the greater probability; his inability to explain the anomaly simply enough for them to understand or their disdain for being talked down to by a scientist a third their age. In either case the man who was sold on his idea was the Marine Corps Commandant, the man whom Alex figured on being the hardest sell.

"Young man do you honestly expect us to sit here and entertain the idea that this General Neutronov and his so called Atomic Army et al, sight unseen, are the biggest threat to our nation's liberty and pursuit of happiness?" Air Force General Shelby Curtis's condescension was so thick that it came across as disgust. Curtis was so plump that he appeared to be stuffed into his dress uniform. Along with a very short comb over and pale complexion he had the appearance of Foghorn Leghorn.

Alex bristled at being treated like a child. His scientific opinions had been well regarded for years. "Yes general that is exactly what I am saying. The President, most of the cabinet, and the entire Secret Service detail witnessed the threat along with me."

Eyes turned as the heavy door of the chamber opened and General Jack Munroe entered. He carried a steel briefcase, which was handcuffed to his wrist. Alex and General Wolf stood up and Wolf began clearing a spot for his longtime friend.

"Thanks Mark, but today I'm on this side of the table. From what I'm hearing, you're on this side too." Munroe cast a stiff brow at the comical looking Curtis.

Admiral Lykins bristled and like any attorney, JAG or otherwise he had a ready argument to support his stance on the matter at hand. The third stooge, the Army Chief of Staff sat quietly watching the unfolding scene as if he were assessing tactical advantage.

As Admiral Lykins went on and Curtis took his side, General Wolf stood up and symbolically slid his file across the able to an empty chair to the right of Alex and as far from the other chiefs as he could get and still be seated at the table.

"Well Frank?" Wolf demanded of the Army chief, who aside from his impressive choice of uniform decoration, made no rash decisions.

General Jackson looked at Wolf and then shot the other two a bored look, "I for one would like to hear what the kid has to say about what went on last night."

"Wonderful, now Stonewall Jackson is the great listener." Curtis quipped with Lykins nodding rapidly in agreement.

Munroe recapped the nights events with a quick and succinct timeline approach meant to neutralize as many of the staff level bureaucrat's stall tactics as possible.

At the end of Munroe's account, Jackson steepled his fingers and sat back in his chair, thoughtfully drumming them against his chin. Finally he asked, "What did you have in mind?"

"Holy smokes, I thought you'd never ask." Alex nodded at Munroe who laid the heavy steel briefcase on the table and thumbed the combination lock.

Munroe opened the case and turned it to Alex who sat out the small ECM device which POPS had built. He also handed Munroe a set of earmuffs. To the others he tossed several sets of GI earplugs on the table.

"What's this?" Curtis demanded.

Alex flipped a switch and turned a knob on another device contained within the briefcase. As soon as he did so the indicator lamp on the ECM began to pulse a bright cherry red.

"I'm sure you'll understand in a minute," Wolf growled as he screwed an earplug into each ear.

Around that moment everyone in the room without the good sense to use the hearing protection began to feel the effects of sound pressure and all off them shifted uncomfortably in their chairs. Alex recognized the first symptom of the sonic weapon.

It started with Curtis who suddenly began to fidget like an addict. Admiral Lykins was next with an uncontrollable itch. The final man to succumb was Jackson who smiled around gritted teeth and reached for the nearest set of ear plugs.

Curtis jumped to his feet and bolted for the door, but General Wolf blocked his way. "Sit down! This will be over in a minute."

Curtis glared at him with hatred in his eyes as he doubled over and sank to his knees. Alex flipped a switch and the test ceased. "Okay gentlemen, that test was with the electronic counter measure turned on. It is not a perfect solution and our assessment concludes that your men will have only as long as it takes for the enemy to figure out the range of our machine and adjust accordingly."

"I don't understand how this little box is going to help. I'm not sure this is even a concern. Our communications monitoring equipment is built by SOS and it didn't pick up on this threat until after it happened. For all we you know and that giant robot of yours could be behind this atomic army," Admiral Lykins accused Alex, his argument supported by the recovering Curtis.

"The hell you say!" Munroe roared as he leapt to his feet and glowered over Lykins. "Alex Conroy, and his father and mother have been stalwart supporters of this nation, through its darkest days. I would and have willingly trusted my life to him on a number of occasions." Munroe leaned far over the conference table, threatening both Lykins and Curtis.

Alex was not alone in thinking that Munroe was about to knock some sense into the pair. General Wolf managed to insert himself between Munroe and them. "Jack, I find his assertions as distasteful as you do, but the tactician in me can't help but conclude that we need to look at other contractors. Specifically those who have had recent troubles or whose leadership is not so... irreproachable." It was Wolf's way of allowing Munroe's honor to be served and spare Curtis the knuckle sandwich he so desperately deserved.

" SIT DOWN!
THIS WILL BE OVER IN A MINUTE. "

"Get a hold of every photographer who was at the White House that night, get every picture taken and identify every man and woman in them. Run down every one of them and you'll find him." Lykins offered.

Munroe sank back into his seat and bit the end off a cigar, "That will take weeks. This Neutronov and his army could strike at any time. Alert the FBI and Secret Service to start combing through their contractors." He glanced at Wolf as he lit the cigar. He drew in a long draught and then glared across the table at Lykins and Curtis, and exhaled, "The same for DON and DAF. I'm leaving here for DOD and then stopping by the Agency. If there are dirty drawers in your closets gentleman they better not be on this skeleton."

"So we're going to pursue this as a disgruntled employee?" Curtis asked in disbelief as he waved off Munroe's exhaust.

"No, but we're leaving no stone unturned." Munroe started

"Making sure all the General's rocks are painted red, white, and blue on the bottom." Wolf growled.

Lykins and Curtis glanced at each other as if they were humoring an old codger. Wolf roared at them, "No one is above suspicion. Guard yourselves and your credibility, there is a traitor who wants to watch Camelot burn."

Alex tossed and turned in a fitful, distressed sleep. He tumbled from the cot to the floor of his office and was suddenly wide awake. As he got to his feet POPS was at the door, "Are you all right, Alex?"

Alex grimaced in the darkness, "Yes, I'm fine POPS." But he wasn't. The surreal dream was still with him and his analytical mind was trying to extrapolate every detail. He contemplated the clock which read 3:18 am.

The phone began to ring and POPS asked, "Shall I answer it?"

Alex opened the door of his office, "No I'll get it. Would you gather data on all competitive defense contractors?"

"Business at this hour?" POPS asked as Alex reached for the phone.

"Hello Jack," Alex said into the phone.

The sound of helicopter rotor blades buffeting filled his ear and Jack Munroe's voice was barely more than a static filled whisper, "Kid we're taking Alamo to the Gast Haus, the nation is under attack."

"General? What happened?" Alex asked, alarmed.

"An aircraft of unknown origin entered US airspace from the front door. It was like some kind of beehive. A cloud of—" The phone squelched. After a burst of static, "—entire Revolution campaign map." The static and squelch again and the sound faded. Munroe's final message, "It's up to you Ghost Boy." The line squelched again and went dead.

"General? Jack!" Alex yelled into the phone. He spun around as the receiver hit the cradle, "POPS!"

"Alex, communications have been lost, but I am still tracking the beacon from both Marine One and Air Force One. They are as you would expect on divergent trajectories away from Washington."

"Monitor all military frequencies as well as law enforcement and emergency channels. I need maps and sit-reps, county by county on both coasts if possible." Alex said as he dressed in his khaki's and combat boots.

"Alex, General Wolf's helicopter has asked for clearance to land on the roof helipad. I've granted it and instructed the pilot to refuel. I assume you'll be taking the General to R&D?"

"Thanks POPS. I need a means of making the average soldier competitive against these drones. Where's the book?" Alex said in one breath.

"No need Alex, your father and George Winkle invented a combat chassis for the military portion of the World of Tomorrow exhibit at the 1949 world fair.

"Why haven't I heard about this?" Alex asked quickly as the romantic vision of rocket propelled infantrymen shot across his imagination.

"Well, the war department ordered enough units for a division, but then as will happen in politics... The other man won." POPS digressed.

Alex momentarily lost his appreciation for the electoral process, but quickly remembered that he had excellent relationships with both the administration and at least one key member of the kitchen cabinet.

"Do we have any?" Alex asked as a distant rumble raised the hair on the back of his neck.

"Yes. The prototype itself was not designed to just grab and go. Due to the tremendous forces exerted on the body, few men could tolerate it. A few of those units are still in inventory, but the majority of them were integrated into a mechanized fighting system for use by cavalry scouts and alongside armor as a new type of mechanized infantry."

Alex held up his hands with impatience on his face, "So where are they and how many?"

The bullet shaped command module lumbered across the Georgetown skyline at a low altitude. The sounds of small arms fire echoed through neighborhoods as armed citizens and police took aim at the slow moving airship.

On the ground a Virginia Army National Guard deuce and a half skidded to a halt between two four story brick buildings. As the nose of the dirigible came into view the driver of the deuce leapt from the cab and he and the passenger pulled the canvas off the truck.

In the bed of the deuce a quad fifty spun on its turret and the gunner unleashed a firestorm from four M-2 .50 caliber machine guns. Tracer bullets marked the path to the command ship, but gave no warning to the gun grew moments later when they returned as elongated darts.

"Incoming!!!" The sergeant yelled as the first of the darts whistled in striking the heavy steal of the truck bed mere inches from his face. The soldiers scrambled for cover beneath the truck or between dumpsters in the alley.

Aside from the terror of incoming fire, the darts returned to earth in an almost musical orchestration of hot metal- *Whunk! Whunk! Whunk! Whunk! Duh-da-da-da-ding! Dah-dun! Whunk!*

Despite the return fire the gunner stayed on target and on the trigger until he succumbed to his wounds. As the men took cover or fell around him, the old sergeant raised his rifle in defiance as a legion of smaller craft began to pour out from the belly of the command ship.

Moments later as the men were crawling from cover and preparing to leave the area the radio in the dart riddled cab squelched to life and a very meek voice said, "Attention all units, this is an all forces priority alert. A G-1 level command authorization is now in effect. The G-1 orders all National Guard, Militia, and Reserve component forces to active service. All personnel are to proceed in the following order of march. All National Guard units are to set up communications and assert command and control. All reserve component units are to report to the nearest State Police barracks and establish field communications relays and initiate operational command posts for theater level command. All regular active duty personnel are recalled from leave if applicable. All personnel are to report to your nearest installation for further orders. Until further notice regional commands are to obey theater order of march. The commander in chief is safe and other leaders are encouraged to shelter in place. All civil defense programs are now initiated. Able bodied men should gather and assist essential services. All veterans are asked to organize pioneer units and report for duty at the nearest military post. Please keep communications channels open for priority communications. Civilian and law enforcement bands may be used for organization and information purposes. Monitor this channel on the quads for updated sit-rep. G-1 out."

In South Williamsport, Pennsylvania the board of directors at SparTacUS (Spartan Tactical Services of the United States) were sitting down to discuss the replacement of Adam Rose their recently deposed founder and chief engineer.

"So here we are," said Treasurer Gary Lynch as he closed the door of the boardroom.

"Yes, here we are. We have convened at your whim, Mr. Lynch." Gayle Howard, said through a stern expression.

Lynch's rodent-like features drew thin as if his chin were the tip of some keel pointed blade, "Whatever do you mean Mr. Howard?"

Being patronized irritated Howard and he stood up, glowering over Lynch, "Don't think for a minute that finding a political way to give the treasurer, you, the final say in boardroom matters somehow relieves you of responsibility for the board's actions, or separates you from its liability."

Lynch was flippant, "No one had an issue with signing the termination of Mr. Rose."

"Adam Rose was a lot of things, but this was his company. The only designs keeping this tub afloat walked out the door with him." Howard countered.

"The old man was off his rocker," Jean Bell the Chief Operations Officer hissed.

"Not to mention that his lab and office in the applied science division has been rendered inaccessible." George Myers the Physical Plant Manager said over his coffee mug.

Lynch wheeled on them, suddenly enraged, "What's gotten into you people? The old man was not the almighty. We legally exercised our right to terminate Adam Rose per by-laws written by him."

"Yes written by an honest, good hearted, sincere man who never dreamed his company, still in its infancy would be snatched from under him by the swami money changer to whom he offered an opportunity where others refused." Howard growled.

Lynch started to rise, "It isn't my fault that when the man incorporated he refused to chair the board or attend its meetings."

Myers attacked this time, "He knew boardrooms were political battlegrounds fraught with silver tongued enemies just like you." He jammed a finger into Lynch's chest. "He knew his personality was better suited to the lab."

"You hold your tongue." Howard shoved him down into a chair. "You sit at this table because he felt sorry for a clerk who was constantly skipped over for promotion. Mr. Adams and I were friends for thirty years before that decision."

Lynch was about to respond when the far wall exploded inward showering the entire boardroom with debris and sending the executives scrambling for cover.

Armed men wearing futuristic composite military fatigues poured through the opening. Lynch ran for the door, but one of the soldiers intercepted him, slinging him into a corner like a crumpled soda can.

They secured the room and only when at least two of the strange rifles covered every board member did the apparent leader step forward, "Gentlemen, one among you is responsible for an act of criminal disloyalty. He will be detained and answer for his crime," the mechanical voice stated.

There was no question that the android troopers were there for Lynch. Not surprising, the executives indicated Lynch with no reservation and moved out of the way, all but Gayle Howard.

Two of the drone troopers seized Lynch and dragged him toward the gaping hole in the wall.

Howard flung his briefcase and then himself at the leader. The briefcase was deflected as if the trooper was swatting a fly. Howard crashed headlong into an invisible field of some kind that protected the leader. As he recovered, Howard threw a heavy crystal vase followed quickly by a coffee carafe and a heavy ceramic cup.

The vase and the carafe were deflected as the briefcase had been, but the ceramic cup slammed squarely into the lead trooper's helmet. The trooper snapped to, raised his rifle and fired an electrostatic pulse which propelled Howard across the room and knocked him unconscious.

Ghost Boy and POPS were supervising a ragtag company of Marines as they familiarized themselves with the SOS Land Warrior Tactical Operations Platform. These men and women had been assembled by General Wolf and they were all that remained of a logistical training battalion. The Land Warrior Weapons System was an enhanced prosthetic which looked like something from a science fiction magazine.

Designed so that when the soldier entered the equipment and strapped in, a couple of hundred touch and motion sensitive contact points would transfer the physical contact to the mechanical interface, thus allowing the soldier or Marine to operate the fighting machine as an extension of him or herself.

The unit came standard with a 7.62mm mini-gun and a belt fed 40mm grenade launcher. Most of the Marines had no trouble learning the interface and in no time they were marching in formation and navigating the obstacles in the freight warehouse and lot with relative ease. In less time the entire company was using the targeting system with deadly precision.

The single stall in the training process was the SCRAM, Self Contained Rocket Assist Module. Leaving the ground was no problem but nearly all of the Marines lost control of the LW on their return to earth. This loss of control included landings on the top or belly of the machine, or the worst, flat on its back, which left both Marine and machine at the most vulnerable.

POPS was in the process of lifting one of the LW's upright when he intercepted a faint transmission from law enforcement to a military liaison. He dropped the LW onto its feet less gently than the Marine inside had expected, but despite protests POPS was already headed toward Ghost Boy. "Alex, Law Enforcement has just relayed a distress call from South Williamsport, Pennsylvania. It seems that this atomic army has attacked the headquarters of Spartan Tactical Services."

"SparTacUS? Holy smokes!" Ghost Boy exclaimed.

"All right Marines, knock off the playtime! We gotta get in this thing. Follow my lead." General Wolf growled over the command channel of his Land Warrior unit. Every unit snapped to attention and fell into formation in front of Wolf.

Wolf turned his LW in a crisp left face and double timed out of the warehouse and into the large open lot before sprinting the length of it, firing and hitting several stacks of pallets with the grenade launcher while on the move. He ran through a series of hand to hand combat moves and activated the SCRAM. As the LW shot skyward he unleashed the mini-gun, sending sawdust flying from yet another stack of pallets. Finally he hovered, gently set down and snapped into a kneeling firing position, bringing both weapons to bear.

Every Marine in the company followed suit. As the last one snapped in and locked on, General Wolf turned to Ghost Boy and raised a huge mechanical arm in salute, "Marine Land Warriors ready to get down to business."

"Great General, next stop SparTacUS." Ghost Boy said with a smile.

The Marines broke into fire teams and moved toward the gates that led out of the lot and onto the main road. Alex and POPS fell in with the command squad behind General Wolf. Security guards closed the gates as the last unit left the lot.

"All secure, Alex," POPS reported to Ghost Boy over their private link.

"Thanks POPS, be sure to keep scanning both radar and communications channels, we don't need any surprises."

"Affirmative Sir," POPS replied.

The column marched onto Interstate 95 and found it nearly deserted. There were no civilian vehicles with the exception of a sparse few commercial trucks. In the first hour there were only minimal military and law enforcement vehicles.

"Looks like a bowling alley after curfew," Sergeant McCoy said over the open channel, drawing frigid laughter from many of his fellow Marines.

Ordinarily Wolf and the other officers would caution him for breaking protocol, but due to the unique nature of the situation, no one elected to enforce form over substance.

General Neutronov sat in the Captain's Chair on the command ship reading one of the vellum smart documents programmed to constantly update the situation reports of his forces.

He looked across the bridge of the airship at the impressive array of technology, most of his own design. His thin lipped smile faded as it settled on him that his impressive toys were packed into such a crude means of transportation.

"General?" A mechanical but feminine voice asked, interrupting his reverie.

"Yes," he snarled at the android in the com station.

"The Mid Atlantic squadron has secured the priority target you're interested in, Sir."

Neutronov brightened, "You don't say?" He rose and went to the com station.

"The detachment has him detained. It seems that there was very little resistance." The electronic voice rasped.

"How far are we from…? Where is it again?" Neutronov asked, as if he didn't know.

"South Williamsport, Pennsylvania, Sir," the definitely female android reported.

"Yes, how far is that?" Neutronov asked.

"Four hundred miles, it will take eight hours from our present location." The navigator reported from an adjacent station.

"Set the course and get out and push." Neutronov groused. His sarcasm was lost on the android.

The convoy of Land Warrior Marines crossed into Pennsylvania moving north on Route 15 in the late evening. The column halted three miles outside the town of Duncannon on the Susquehanna River. The lead squad secured the route of march while the second and third squads secured the flanks.

General Wolf's voice came over the command channel, "Fourth platoon, recon the town. You know the drill. First platoon will provide support. The main element will move up as you clear."

"Yes Sir." The fourth platoon moved forward in a phalanx toward the edge of town.

An hour of radio silence had passed when General Wolf again came on the command channel, "Recon team status update over?"

"It's quiet, Sir. No dogs barking, no birds chirping. No people."

"Affirmative, continue your mission."

Sergeant Sharp signaled his squad to spread out. As they did so, Sharp scanned his lane for any sign of life. The recon element advanced to the city center. After a moment's observation Sergeant Sharp went to the center of the main intersection. He scanned 360 degrees and radioed, "Command One, this is Recon One. The town appears deserted. Please send up a team to check municipal buildings and locate the civil defense plan."

⋮ ⋮

Ghost Boy heard the request for a team to enter buildings on foot and he turned to POPS, "That's our cue."

"On your mark, Alex." The metal giant said as he stepped forward.

Ghost Boy led a squad of LW Marines to the town center. POPS scanned with both radar and sonar to no avail. Ghost Boy climbed the steps to the court house as the Marines dismounted their land warrior units.

In the lobby of the court house he searched the directory for the city engineer's office. He found it and crossed the lobby in search of the stairwell that led down to the basement. He passed through the rotunda and grabbed the tarnished brass rail at the top of the stairs. He paused, reflecting on the unnaturalness of the silence. The hair on the back of his neck tingled as he started down the steps.

The steep marble staircase led to a suite of offices that had been built on the cheap with modular construction. He smelled the musty dampness of a newly renovated space and behind it, the musk masked urine scent of fear. He heard nothing but the hum of a Coke machine. He slowly passed the title agency and the recorder's office. He shoved a hand into his pocket for a quarter and pushed it into the coin slot of the Coke machine.

He felt a shift in the air aside from the rush of cold air when he opened the door of the Coke machine to pull out a ten ounce glass bottle. His keen sense allowed him to feel some unseen person's movements, but aside from opening the bottle of Coke, he didn't react. Someone or something was moving beyond the corner at the end of the hall near the Civil Planning office.

Slowly he crept to the end of the hall, confident that he was sensing the presence of another person. He didn't hear breathing and found the presence without respiration to be slightly unnerving. Alex went invisible as a shadow broke around the corner of the hallway. A middle aged man in a white oxford shirt and black trousers stepped around the corner and then retreated.

Ghost Boy relaxed and became visible, "Sir, I'm here with a detachment of Marines."

For a long moment the man neither moved nor spoke. Ghost Boy was about to move when the man rounded the corner, aggressively brandishing a chromed ceremonial shovel. "Yeah, what assurance do I have that you're not one of them?"

"Sir, outside you'll find a company of mechanized Marines led by a staff level officer. He gathered what marines he could find and came to me for equipment. I'm Alex Conroy, I'm looking for the town's civil defense plan. Do you know where the townspeople are taking shelter?" The man sized him up, noticing specifically the way he avoided making sudden movement

"It's here in my office, I'm Clark Schaefer, the city engineer. In a small town though you wear about a dozen other hats and get volunteered for a lot of hey-you type jobs." He gestured toward the open doorway.

Schaefer walked around the counter and laid out two binders from the shelf below, "Here's our disaster plan, but it won't do you a lot of good."

Ghost Boy tilted his head slightly, trying to discern whether or not the man was being intentionally deceptive, "Meaning what exactly?"

The fellow's irritation was thick in his voice, evident in his clinched jaw. "Well it was an all fired government hurry up and wait. They fined the city for not having a plan drawn up to their specifics. So we got one, and don't you know they approved the plan and not a nickel of the funding to put it in place."

Ghost Boy nodded. "That misfortune may have made you the wisest town managers on the east coast,"

"People are scared to death and we can't afford to feed them. The Sheriff's office is shuttling families to clear out their iceboxes and larders, so I guess we're also running the biggest soup kitchen."

Ghost Boy nodded and put a hand on the man's shoulder, "If you can take us there, I can get you some assistance." He wasn't sure the man would take him up on the offer.

"How do you plan to do that? You said yourself that the Marines you're with are just a few stragglers." Schaefer sounded skeptical.

Ghost Boy grinned, "We're pretty resourceful people. I need to get back topside, so if you're taking us to the shelter, we need to be on our way. The Marines are headed for South Williamsport and won't abide much of a delay."

"Must be pretty bad up there. I heard one of the deputies relaying

" ALEX WENT INVISIBLE AS A SHADOW
BROKE AROUND THE CORNER OF THE HALLWAY. "

information. I guess a bunch of those spacemen attacked a powder factory or something." Schaefer said as he returned the binders to the shelf.

Detecting the man's interest and apprehension, Ghost Boy said, "I'd be lying if I told you that we weren't going for that very reason."

"I'll take you to the camp," Schaefer said and followed Ghost Boy toward the stairs.

∷ ∷
∷

The Land Warrior Marines followed the city engineer's truck out of town. A couple of miles west of Duncannon the truck turned onto a primitive track meant for heavy mining and earthmoving equipment. The truck slowed drastically to navigate the trail, which was only a road in the loosest sense.

The Land Warrior units of the Marines had no trouble at all navigating the rugged terrain. Ever resourceful they soon discovered that using the SCRAM to assist they could readily sprint up the steep grade past the truck. They poured through the manmade pass and into the expansive strip mined moonscape. As they did so each squad moved to secure the quad.

Third Squad, led by Staff Sergeant Kendrick was the last group through the pass. They moved directly to secure the opening of the cave. As the point unit closed within one hundred feet of the cave opening, the sound of a high powered rife echoed across the tract.

"Please hold your fire. This is Staff Sergeant Thomas Kendrick, United States Marine Corps."

Silence followed and several tense moments passed before anyone within the dark cave opening moved. Finally, Schaefer the engineer went to the opening and called out to someone. A moment later an old man limped out of the cave, supporting himself on a spud bar. He carried a model 1903 Springfield rifle slung on his shoulder.

"Sheriff Garrett these men are Marines, the Ghost Boy is with them," Schaefer said as the old fellow came into view.

The Sheriff looked across the quad at the Marines and their machines, "I'm sad to say we can't feed them, they'll have to go."

"You don't need to Sheriff. Is there anything we can do for you or your people?" Ghost Boy asked as he arrived at the cave entrance.

"From what I can tell this atomic army is trying to make a statement.

Aside from the capitol they're hitting targets that don't make a lot of military sense."

"How do you mean?" Ghost Boy asked.

"Well, Block Island, Saratoga, and Breed's Hill… Those are national landmarks, not strategic points." The Sheriff said as if everyone should have known.

"Holy Smokes," Ghost Boy said on his way to tell General Wolf.

Security personnel at Spartan Tactical Services were still reeling from the earlier attack by the atomic army's drone troopers. When the first elements of the Land Warrior Marines arrived at the closed security checkpoint the two uniformed security guards fled their post, refusing to stop even after the marines identified themselves. After a cursory recon of the area the marines opened the gate.

Ghost Boy and POPS arrived at the gate just ahead of the secondary marine elements and entered the complex.

"Alex, I'm certain you've seen the damaged building up ahead. I am detecting a dozen different body heat signatures." POPS said as they went along.

"Thanks POPS. You better let me go in there first." Ghost Boy replied and double timed toward the headquarters building.

Ghost Boy detected the racing thoughts of several men and women within the darkened structure. POPS took up a security position and waited.

After listening for several moments Ghost boy went to the gaping tear in the building's façade and disappeared inside. "Hello?" He called out as he entered the dark structure into what was once a conference room. He called out a number of times but no one acknowledged him. As he moved through the room he heard the sounds of labored respiration coming from the far corner of the room, behind an overturned credenza.

As he walked toward the credenza, a sudden rush of air telegraphed the movements of someone large who slipped on a loose manila folder in the debris strewn room and slid headlong into a pile at Ghost Boy's feet.

Instinctively he took up a defensive stance but when the man turned over, he cringed. The man started to retreat as Alex bent over him.

He spoke to the man gently saying, "Sir, I'm Alex and I'm here to help you." He extended a hand to the timid fellow.

The man cowered as Alex made another attempt. A woman's voice behind said, "He's suffered a psychological break." Alex looked toward the overturned credenza, searching for the source of the voice.

Alex left the man for a moment and went to the corner of the room. He moved the credenza and helped the woman to her feet. "What can you tell me about what happened?" He asked as she steadied herself against him.

"We were having a meeting on the succession. They blew open the wall and just took him." She exclaimed.

"Succession?" Ghost Boy asked.

"Yes, Mr. Lynch and Mr. Henderson were arguing over the assertion that it was almost too convenient that our founder and chief engineer was suddenly let go after he and Lynch had a falling out." She explained.

"So Mr. Lynch is the chairman?" Ghost Boy asked as he helped her to a chair.

"No, Henderson is the chairman, but Lynch held such sway with the old man. He was somehow able to have the articles changed so that the treasurer held final say."

"He's treasurer?" He asked for confirmation.

She nodded, "This is not the first time he's manipulated the system to his advantage."

He raised an eyebrow, "What does that mean, exactly?"

"Lynch was a clerk. For years. A man with no future and a dead end job. It was our founder Adam Rose who promoted him, and against the advice of the board I might add. Lynch moved from clerk to staff accountant to supervisor, to controller, to CFO in a blink. We have a policy preventing job hopping, but it didn't apply to Mr. Rose's projects."

Alex didn't need his enhanced perception to pick up on the notes of sarcasm and envy in her voice. He didn't need keen powers of observation to know that this woman had also spent time on a median rung of the corporate ladder. It must have been difficult for her to watch an incompetent race to where her hard work had only kept her in the slow lane.

"Where is everyone?" Ghost Boy asked, sensing that the fellow who'd been on the floor had left through the hole in the wall.

She was quiet for a long moment, "Most of them headed home to see about their families. Henderson is still here, he went to lock up."

Ghost Boy, thinking she was in shock said, "Holy Smokes, this is a big place to lock up."

She smiled at him as if he were being sarcastic, "Yes it would be. We have an army of security for that, but every afternoon Mr. Henderson spins a report and locks the reels from the computer in the vault.

"Let's go find him," Ghost Boy said quickly, trying to move her along. She nodded and turned on her heel, leading him toward the door of the conference room.

After a quick introduction Henderson gave Ghost Boy a further recounting of the events that had taken place when Lynch was taken.

"Is there anything else?" He asked as they walked out into the afternoon sun.

"Only that I threw my briefcase at them and it was deflected somehow. But the funny thing is, I threw a coffee mug and it passed right through whatever that shielding is and cracked him square on the helmet."

Alex tilted his head slightly and asked, "What material was it made of; stoneware, ceramic, glass?

Henderson stepped inside momentarily and returned with a cobalt colored mug bearing the Spartan Tactical logo, "They're made of a high velocity ceramic polymer, the same material we use in an experimental lead free projectile."

"Holy smokes! Do you think Adam Rose would be capable of this?" Trying to contain his interest in his competitor's achievements.

"I want to say no," Henderson started.

Ghost Boy caught his hesitation immediately. He looked into the man's eyes and asked, "But?"

"Well, Adam wasn't a boardroom and business suit guy. He was a man who built weapons and developed better ones. He was living the cold war in his mind and in his lab at all times. When the man he rescued from obscurity all but stole the company he built up from a simple improvement on one piece of hardware to being the world's largest military contractor, it was more than he could take." Henderson replied at length.

Alex listened and began to suspect that Adam Rose might have truly been a victim, but of whom? "Thank you. We have to stop this, but we will take into account that Rose might be pursuing what he might view as an equivalent response."

"He's a good man," Henderson added as Ghost Boy started to depart, causing him to stop short.

Something about Henderson was off. Ghost Boy tried to read his thoughts, but found it to be a cacophony of chaos, quite understandable for the place and time. He opted to try another tack, "Do you have any of his notes or drawings. This shield system is something we are unprepared for." A sudden change in Henderson's respiration and heart rate caused Ghost Boy to go on alert. "If there is anything you want to tell us that will help subdue the threat, the better this will end." He was pleased to see Henderson take note of the less than gentle edge in his voice.

POPS approached quickly, followed by General Wolf who was flanked by a pair of Land Warrior units. Henderson looked at the seven foot tall silver robot and grimaced, "We have not exactly been able to get into his lab since he left. He had some sort of biometric lock installed and... Well I've been hesitant to let anyone just cut their way in."

Ghost Boy caught another spike in his pulse, he was beginning to get a much clearer picture of who Henderson was, "Maybe we can help." He offered and turned to POPS.

"Yes, Alex?" POPS said.

They were headed inside when POPS spun quickly around and tilted his head skyward. Servos whirred and hydraulics hissed while unseen electronic processes ran silently. Having located some as yet unseen object POPS emitted a single ping.

Ghost Boy knew before the robot spoke. "General, tell your men to prepare their defenses. Be ready for their sonic weapon." To Henderson and the lady, whose name he'd learned was Joyce Cummins, "The both of you are going to need heavy duty hearing protection and..."

"Their weapons emit an electrostatic pulse," Henderson cut him off.

POPS head turned, followed by his body, "Alex, I detect a slow moving airship. A dirigible of some type and a number of much smaller craft also slow moving. Their range is just over ten miles."

"What?" Henderson demanded and Ghost Boy gently turned him and moved him toward the door.

"We need to get into Rose's lab now," Ghost Boy said moving him forward until he started moving on this own. Henderson reached for the door but Joyce beat him to it. She let the door swing closed behind POPS and then sat down on a low retaining wall.

Behind her the Land Warrior Marines were taking up fighting positions, moving cars or turning them over to create a scatter field of irregular shapes to help hide their fighting machines from both human and electronic eyes.

POPS scanned the biometric lock while Ghost Boy examined its electronic panel. After a moment the robot said, "Alex, this is next generation security. It is not only biometric, but requires a manual pass-code entry."

"Great," Henderson fumed, "Why didn't I fire Lynch when I condemned him to the dock?"

Ghost Boy listened to Henderson's going on for over a minute before he tuned him out by turning his attention to POPS, "What do you make of its innards?" POPS turned its head and a pneumatic cylinder hissed. It sounded like a disgusted sigh, Ghost Boy concurred with the feeling but didn't speak.

"For all its impressive architecture I don't believe it is well insulated. Very possibly it could be shorted open."

Alex lifted the cover of the electronic panel and traced a finger over the schematic. He stopped at the serial bus. He traced it again and then shook his head. "Why bother? POPS, go ahead and short it, and it should open. It doesn't appear to have a parallel or duplex circuit anywhere."

"Stand by for static discharge." POPS extended a huge hand and inserted a probe into a port on the keypad. Static electricity discharged through the system and the smell of ozone rose until the air felt dry and brittle. POPS grounded against a bolt head and the resulting arc blew the entire panel, bridging all of the current controlled switches. Something within the heavy steel door released with a metallic click and the lever appeared to relax as if tension had been relieved.

Ghost Boy ushered Henderson out of the way and examined the lever's mechanism before trying it. When he pushed down on the lever the heavy spring within groaned and the latch retracted with a loud bang, startling him and causing Henderson to cower.

"Holy Smokes," Ghost Boy exhaled.

POPS pushed the heavy door inward, groaning on its hinges. He entered the lab followed by Ghost Boy. Henderson waited until they were well inside before he set foot in the lab.

Ghost Boy flipped a switch. The lights came up on an almost antiseptically clean research and development lab. The floors, tables and even the tools were immaculately clean. Ghost Boy also noticed that every workstation was mechanically organized, something only a person who worked with a robot might notice.

Further inspection showed signs of both genius and obsessive compulsion. It was evident that Adam Rose had been living in his lab. His office was furnished like a tiny apartment. "Boy, talk about not getting out much," Henderson scoffed, leaning into the office, but not actually walking inside. "You could eat off the floors and work tables in the shop, but I wouldn't eat an astronaut's diet in that office."

POPS moved past the drafting table where Ghost Boy was leafing through an extensive stack of drawings on blueprint paper, many of them with complete diagrams and exploded views of internal mechanisms drawn on onion skin and attached as overlays. The scent of mimeograph ink assaulted his nose and he turned away from the table just as a sneeze erupted.

Henderson met him as he turned back to the drafting table, "What is it you're looking for exactly?"

"Plans or an abstract that will tell us how to neutralize the threat." Ghost Boy said a bit less gently than the fellow was expecting.

"Neutralize... You don't mean to kill him?" Henderson sounded shocked.

"I'd prefer that it not come to that, but we have to be prepared. Do you have any ammunition with that ceramic projectile?" Ghost Boy asked, knowing that General Wolf would press the question.

Henderson nodded, appreciating the interest, "The usual, fifty BMG and seven-six-two. We even have a couple of thousand 40mm for the thumpers."

Ghost Boy was about to ask Henderson about Rose's research assistants when POPS returned, "Alex, every workspace is set up identically.

"Robots?"

"Yes, and not crude." POPS affirmed.

"No, we have only prototyped simple robotics. The troops who seized Lynch were not the stuff from the CAD lab." Henderson insisted.

"CAD lab?" Ghost Boy asked.

"Combat Action Developers. They build and test equipment for use under live fire conditions." Henderson answered with his best salesman's smile.

"You say the drone troopers used electrostatic weapons? I don't suppose you have any of those lying around?" Ghost Boy asked with a note of sarcasm.

"I'm afraid not. I doubted the viability of that technology. That is until earlier today." Henderson said, stopping quickly as if he'd let slip a detail he shouldn't have. Neither Ghost Boy nor POPS let on that they'd heard.

"General Wolf's Marines would appreciate some of that ceramic ammunition." Ghost Boy said absently.

Henderson nodded and turned to leave the lab. As he did so Ghost Boy started searching through the drawings again.

"Alex, by my calculations the Atomic Army's command ship should be within four miles of our location." POPS offered.

"Holy Smokes! I need to get on that command ship." Ghost Boy exhaled as he pulled a drawing off the stack. He turned it around and thumped it with a finger. "POPS take a look at that."

POPS turned and the servos in his neck and camera sockets whirred. "This is the schematic for an electrostatic pulse weapon. In this case, a rifle."

"Look at the project approval." Ghost Boy pointed.

"Gayle Henderson." POPS said, his mechanical tone sounding like an indictment.

"Interesting, aye?" Ghost Boy said as he rolled the drawing, "Let's go. We need to get out there and let General Wolf know what's going on. I need to get on that command ship."

"Very, well, I do not like it," POPS followed him out of the lab.

Outside General Wolf was setting up his Marines like the pieces on a chess board. It was evident to Ghost Boy that Wolf was completely in his element. The Land Warrior unit he drove simply underscored Wolf's bigger than life marine's marine persona. "General, I need to brief you on a bit of critical information."

Paul Lynch was frog marched onto the main deck of the airship and brought before the commander.

"So you are the usurper Lynch? It was on your authority that my master was to be dismissed." The large android's mechanical voice condemned through a mirthless and unmoving smile.

"Adam Rose put you up to this?" Lynch demanded, his beady eyes and angry expression failing to crack the android's blank expression.

"Our master created us to serve," it rasped.

"So he ordered you to kidnap me?" Lynch's temper flared as he tried again to assert himself.

"The creator must be protected. Our master must be served. Take him away." Strong hands seized Lynch and marched him to a storage cage on the lowest deck.

Despite Lynch's protests or attempts to bargain the drone troopers did not respond or relent. They deposited him in the cage, closed and locked the door, then walked away.

"You can't leave me here. I'm an important man. My company will pay or trade for my release." He called after them.

From behind him, in a dark corner a small voice said, "I'm afraid you can't bargain with them. They possess no conscience. They know only duty and allegiance to the cold structure of programmed orders."

Lynch turned, "How would you know?" He demanded of the timid, vaguely familiar voice.

"Because I designed them that way." The fellow said quietly as he stepped into the light.

"Mr. Rose, what are you doing here?" Lynch asked, stunned.

"I'd ask you the same, but considering you had it in your mind to take something you had no right to…you belong here. Considering that I built all of this, so do I. But it appears that we were both duped, by someone else." Rose replied in a mechanical tone reminiscent of the command troopers.

"So you ordered this attack? Do you have any idea what is happening?" Lynch attempted to take the moral high ground.

"I gave them everything except the ability to feel. In their minds, as complex and simple as they are, it is reasonable to them that by keeping me imprisoned here and destroying everything with which I have ever shown the slightest dismay…" Rose trailed off.

Lynch looked at him with both pity and horror. Two emotions that were new to him. He'd never had anything, let alone anything to lose. Never mind anything worth having. The man in front of him had given him everything, and now it was all gone. Everything, his life for all he knew, gone. "So here we are."

Rose glared at him, anger boiling over. "You and I might be confined to the same cage at the current time, but there is not now, nor will there be in the future a version of we involving the two of us in any context. You may have quietly found a way to push me out of the company I built and in which you have no stake, but it is still mine. I own the majority of voting shares." Rose was seething, "Since money and power are what you understand, wrap your over reaching mind around this; if you make it out of here alive I will be buying back all of the shares and taking my company private. You will be sanctioned and terminated, then prosecuted to the fullest extent of the law."

"So you're angry that you were let go." Lynch hissed, his blasé tone further enraging Rose. "What did you expect when you stopped working and became a recluse?"

" MR. ROSE, WHAT ARE YOU DOING HERE ? "

Rose surged out of the corner and attacked. He closed a hand around Lynch's throat and slammed him against the wall of the cage.

"You cannot arm those who wish to do us harm with the finest tools of the trade. We don't do business that way. We never have, or needed to." Rose yelled. He slung Lynch away as if discarding garbage. He went back to his corner and retrieved a number of strange looking electronic components which appeared to have been hastily cobbled together. He somehow fastened one to another, assembling some sort of device.

"What is that?" Lynch asked trying to assert himself.

"Wouldn't you like to know," Rose asked as he raised the weapon.

On the ground the Marines prepared to defend against a technologically superior enemy. Wolf had given the only speech he had. He did his best to inspire his marines and now it was up to them to take their training and apply guts and determination.

"General I need to get on that airship. Maybe I can disable it and bring it down." Ghost Boy drew Wolf's attention to the command ship on the horizon.

"You mean that metal behemoth can't just throw you up there?" Wolf chuckled.

"He probably could but I was thinking I'd hitch a ride on an LW and use the SCRAM to catapult me up there.

"I can levitate, but I can't fly so a push would be a big help." Ghost Boy said as he tied down a belt knife he'd borrowed from a marine.

"Do you want a sidearm or a rifle?" Wolf asked as if yes were the only correct answer.

"No I don't use guns. The knife is a last resort for bringing that thing down." Ghost Boy said as he stood up.

"We're as ready as we are going to be. Use caution, but understand that we have no choice here but to stop the threat to our nation. Adam Rose or Paul Lynch, or whomever is behind this has to be brought to justice." Wolf said, as he glared at the airship looming closer.

Ghost Boy agreed, "Let's hope it goes in our favor, but if not hit them with everything. Remember that something in that shield technology distorts ball ammo so if you fire on it, you may get it back as those darts.

Henderson is supposed to get us some ceramic ammo, but I haven't seen him since he left the lab. Remember those drones are not to be trifled with."

"Neither are we!" Wolf growled.

"No, but we're rational and bound by the laws of land warfare. We don't know anything about Adam Rose's mental state, or if Lynch is really his prisoner, or that Rose may not be in command." Ghost Boy countered.

"According to Henderson," Wolf started.

"Like I said, I'm not so sure Henderson is as forthcoming with information as he would like us to believe." Alex explained to Wolf about finding Henderson's endorsement on the design he professed to know nothing about.

"I can't say I'm surprised, but I think he gets the benefit of the doubt for the time being because I don't need another headache. I've considered that Rose and Henderson might be in this together but Lynch doesn't have the guts to do anything but over reach the gravy bowl. We'll sort him out later."

A radio squelched and a young voice reported, "Command One, this is team one actual. Sitrep as follows. Team one is in place and ready." In succession the other fire teams called in their respective situation reports.

Wolf was thoughtful before calling over the command channel, "Land Warriors, I need Staff Sergeant Johansen and one high speed fire-baller from every team at fire control ASAP."

Wolf looked at Ghost Boy and said, "I'm going to get you up there and I'm sending some of my best people with you."

As soon as Johansen arrived General Wolf briefed him on the mission and in turn he and Ghost Boy relayed the message to the others when they were assembled. As Ghost Boy was about to depart with the marines POPS came up to him, "Be careful, Alex."

"Thanks POPS. Do anything you can to mitigate their sonic weapon or that shield. If we fail you know what to do." Ghost Boy said, looking on the robot with the affection a boy might have for his father.

"I do indeed, Alex, but it will not come to that. You are quite clever if I may so." The robot sounded sentimental.

"Okay Marines, saddle up." Johansen's husky voice commanded.

"I gotta go POPS," Ghost Boy said before he sprinted to catch up with the Land Warriors.

The Land Warriors stopped in a copse of trees in the city park. Johansen had advanced the team to the place where the airship had been sighted before disappearing behind near objects which occluded the horizon.

"Command this is Advance Actual," Johansen called over the radio.

"Go advance," Wolf replied.

"Command, Intel said that drones poured out of that thing when it was fired on. Would we have a better chance if the hive was empty when we try to steal the honey?" Johansen asked.

"Hold one advance." Wolf replied, followed with, "How many on your team?"

"Six plus one," Johansen answered.

Wolf replied, "Affirmative Advance, six plus one. Your call."

"Command, Advance Actual standing by to attack on your mark." Johansen replied. He signaled the group to rally on his position and said to them without broadcasting, "Here's the deal, we're going to hit that thing with HE just before we send the Ghost Boy. We need to get as many of those things engaged as possible to give him a change to get in, and shut that thing down."

"Advance Actual, this is Command. You have a mark." Wolf gave the order to attack. The radio squelched and fell silent.

All eyes were on Johansen, who raised the right hand of his LW and clenched the mechanical hand into a fist, "All right Marines. Let's get it done."

Ghost Boy stilled himself and listened intently. In the distance there was the hum of a generator and beneath that the sound of a propeller. Just under that noise, he detected also the murmur of electronics. He spoke to POPS via their private link. "POPS do you see that ship on radar?"

"Yes. It is still moving, though not fast. It has not slowed. I detect no active radar, though there is a Doppler signature, so remain concealed until you are ready to make your move. Given the present speed and heading the airship will close on your position within the hour.

"Thanks POPS. Continue to monitor and if there's a change or drones start deploying before we engage, let me know ASAP." Ghost Boy said quickly.

Johansen dismounted his LW and came over to where Ghost Boy was standing. "Sir," he began to say but Ghost Boy held up a hand.

"Don't call me Sir. My name is Alex, or Ghost Boy is fine as well."

Johansen nodded, "Force of habit. I just wanted to talk. Something about all this doesn't add up."

Alex listened to the big man's words and also his heartbeat and respiration. He reflected momentarily on the man's calm, "What doesn't add up?"

Johansen cleared his throat and spat, "Well, based on what I've seen, and two stories one painting a picture of him as an over reaching pencil pusher, and the other as a cold ambitious opportunist out to take a better man's company. I don't see anything worth all the trouble. Somebody needs to get into the Henderson's background. What about that woman who just happened to be hiding behind a desk when you got in there?"

"I mentioned the same thing to General Wolf." Alex confided in him, glad to know that he wasn't alone in his suspicion of Henderson. But he'd missed the probability of the woman's involvement. "I missed it on Joyce."

Johansen took Ghost Boy's radio and tuned it to the command channel, "Command this is Advance actual, over."

"Go Advance," Wolf answered.

Johansen glanced at Ghost Boy who nodded his encouragement. "Command watch your six, we have reason to believe that we got bad intel from the local Honcho."

"Affirmative Advance, we'll play it close to the vest." Wolf replied.

Johansen was about to sign off when the shadow of the airship came into view, "Command its show time, Advance out."

Johansen ran to his LW and mounted the vehicle followed by Ghost Boy who sprang onto the top of the unit. Johansen gave the signal and all eyes were on him. "On my mark send up HE, proximity burst only."

As the rear of the command ship passed overhead the open cargo bay was visible and Ghost Boy pointed it out to Johansen.

"Ready, mark!" Johansen raised the automatic grenade launcher on his LW and targeted the airship. He fired a three round burst and the weapon continued to track. The others followed suit and their grenades shot skyward exploding in proximity to the dirigible. Showers of sparks erupted, no visible damage was done, but it did elicit a reaction.

"Alex?" POPS called Ghost Boy over their private channel.

"Yes POPS?" He answered.

"The Doppler signature was not radar at all. It has to be the signature of their shield device. When the Marines fired their weapons, the Doppler rippled and lit up at every point where a projectile exploded. I can't speak to the shrapnel but the kinetic energy of the explosive definitely hit the mark."

"Holy smokes! Thanks POPS." He said and the relayed the information to Johansen.

"So we should take out anything that looks like an antenna?" Someone asked.

"Affirmative, domes, dishes, or vanes." Johansen replied.

He looked at the airship and was saying, "Hit it again." When the first drones began to emerge. "Hold fire! Hold fire!"

The drones continued to pour out for nearly a minute. Johansen couldn't believe his eyes. "Fire!" He sent another burst from his grenade launcher and the team followed suit.

The grenades exploded amidst the drones and again the concussion had greater affect than the shrapnel, disabling some, knocking others out of the sky altogether. As the last of them emerged from the airship, they began to rally.

"Fire at will." Johansen ordered and the squad fired targeted bursts at the cluster of drones. As the grenades exploded around them disturbing their attempt to organize Johansen yelled, "Attack!"

The Land Warrior marines leapt skyward using their SCRAMs and took the fight to their enemy. When the last of them engaged Johansen shot skyward, like a homesick angel. Ghost Boy braced himself, counted off the seconds and called, "Disengage!"

Alex went invisible just as Johansen cut the thrust. As Alex had predicted the thrust carried him on and upward toward the command ship's open cargo bay.

Using levitation to keep himself on target and slow his ascent Ghost Boy realized that he was coming in too fast to safely enter the cargo bay. He swallowed the lump in his throat and in a feat of sheer acrobatic will he rolled in the air, sprung himself off the top of the bulkhead to the low rigging of the airbladder and into the open cargo bay, rolling to his feet in a defensive stance.

The first thing that Ghost Boy noticed was the cleanliness of the cargo bay. There was no dirt, dust, grease, or spilled oil. Tools were hung on fitted boards in a maintenance area. Weapons of various types stood in racks. Alex remained invisible as he levitated toward the rear of the cargo bay. As he floated above a storage cage, he heard anxious men talking.

General Wolf set his jaw as the first sounds of combat echoed across the valley. He hadn't expected the first action he'd seen in twenty years to be in Lady Liberty's own damned backyard.

"Advance Actual, this is Command. Sitrep over." Wolf said over the command channel.

"Command, Advance is engaged with the enemy force. The package has been delivered. We are facing a remaining force of one hundred drones. Grenades are effective by concussion only. Projectiles are useless. How copy over?" Johansen responded.

"Affirmative Advance, good copy. Status of their shield?" Wolf replied.

"Sir, when we get a handle on these drones we will take out the control for the shield barrier."

"Carry on Advance, keep me advised." Wolf directed. He looked toward the horizon. He felt the concussion of the explosions and smelled the dry heat of the sun. Tasted the burnt powder. In his mind he was suddenly a boot lieutenant leading a rifle company on some unnamed island in the Pacific just a few hundred miles from Japan.

The abrupt eruption of chaos behind him was familiar in a way he could never explain. Time slowed as Wolf raised his head from its reverie. He whirled his LW unit around and fired the M2 Browning .50 caliber machine gun at the advancing drones. But where had they come from?

Wolf dashed behind the cover of an overturned truck. The truck was instantly peppered with lightweight shot. Wolf glanced over the truck to gauge the range to the attacking drones and returned fire with the grenade launcher.

Whump! Whump! Whump!

Followed by three explosions.

Wolf heard the squads returning fire before he actually saw it.

As the sound of 40mm grenade launchers was followed by the concussive, bone rattling explosions a legion of drones poured out of the warehouse complex!

With drones falling out of the sky or otherwise engaged, Johansen targeted any protrusion that might have been an antenna in an attempt to disable the shield system. He located a pair of parabolic domes on the belly of the Airship's cargo bay. They were located amidships on either side of a huge power horn speaker. He closed the distance and fired a three round volley.

The first grenade made no impact. The second's concussion triggered a defense mechanism. The sonic weapon chirped to life. No sooner had it begun when the third grenade exploded.

Johansen rolled his LW on its axis to avoid a burst of electrostatic rifle fire. As he turned he watched the first grenade miss and the second trigger the shrill weapon. As he tilted upright he watched the third grenade slam into the chest piece of a drone trooper.

It exploded, propelling the shielded trooper into the antenna array at twenty two thousand feet per second. The man sized armored projectile tore off both parabolic antennae and the loudspeaker.

Johansen watched the whole mess falling to earth in disbelief. He scanned the length of the airship for another antenna, "Advance team one, antenna array down. Let's hit this thing."

Ghost Boy gathered from the conversation between the two men that Rose and Lynch were prisoners and while very angry with each other, they were not bitter enemies. He quietly lowered himself to the floor of the cargo bay and became visible. "I don't suppose the two of you want to stay here?"

Both men hurried to the door of the cage, Lynch proclaiming his innocence and Rose offering his assistance.

"Let me see to this lock," Ghost Boy said as he examined the inset mechanism.

"On the schematic I called for a simple three pin internal residential lock." Rose offered.

Ghost Boy searched his pockets and came up with a tiny screwdriver and a medium weight paperclip, which he quickly fashioned into an L shaped tension wrench.

Ghost Boy made fast work of the lockset's tumbler and as the door swung open he asked Rose, "How do we shut down the shield mechanism and how do we shut down this atomic army of yours?"

Rose frowned at the reference and asked, "If they were mine would I be a prisoner? The quantum shield is generated locally and has a very short range. Two antennae on the top and bottom of the airship and another set on the ground at HQ. There are also beacons for the compliance system, but I believe your people already sorted that out. Luckily most of this technology is prototypical and not fully functional. That includes the troopers, all but the command units. General Neutronov is truly complete, he will be a problem."

"Where is he?" Ghost Boy asked.

"On the command deck," Rose offered.

"Anything else I need to know?" Ghost Boy prepared to move.

"Yes, Gayle Henderson and Joyce Cummins have this maniacal vision of themselves as despotic rulers of a new world order." Lynch insisted and Rose reluctantly concurred.

"Where is engagement control?" Ghost Boy inquired.

"On the ground at Spartan. If you can get me there." Rose offered.

"There are Marines there fighting the drones." Ghost Boy said.

Johansen flew into the cargo bay flanked by two other LW marines, causing Rose and Lynch to retreat. Ghost Boy reassured them, "Those guys are on our side." He turned to Johansen and shared what he'd learned from Rose.

"We'll get you gentlemen on the ground and take the fight back to Spartacus." Johansen said, directing Rose to the nearest LW, followed by Lynch. With the recently liberated prisoners secured, Ghost Boy once again hitched a ride with Johansen.

As Johansen and his men left the cargo bay he radioed the advance team, "Advance team, this is Team Leader. Shift your attack. Take down the Airship and return to Rally Point."

POPS was in the thick of the battle, trying to look after General Wolf. He was also monitoring communications. He shoved a Volkswagen bus at a pair of drones and called Ghost Boy on their private link, "Alex, the number of drone troops is increasing. There is also a very high level of RF radiation emanating from sources separate from the communications tower. One of which is emitting a sub range test pulse. In close monitoring of both I believe it is safe to hypothesize that the drones on the ground are being controlled from within the facility. A particular area of the factory seems to be rather well protected by both drones and the sonic weapon. There is also the shield system to contend with. I detect multiple Doppler signatures, but I cannot triangulate a pattern for jamming."

"Thanks POPS. How's the General faring?" Ghost Boy asked.

"He is taking the fight to them as best he can, but breathing room is becoming scarce." POPS said, sounding unsure.

"If you get the chance apprehend Gayle Henderson and Joyce Cummins. I have Adam Rose and Paul Lynch, both were prisoners aboard the command ship." Ghost Boy said, "Pass the word to destroy all antenna arrays."

Suddenly a dozen drones broke through the line and attacked General Wolf and the command squad. "No time, Alex, they've broken our line and are gaining ground. You must hurry. I have to assist." POPS ended the conversation.

### ∴∴∴

The airship nosed in at a twenty degree angle, erupting into a rolling ball of fire, crumbled metal and fabric. As the fireball dissolved a half dozen war machines became visible driving hard through the smoke. Joined by the forward security team a fresh dozen land warriors were coming in hot and throwing themselves into the fight. 40mm grenades exploded causing drones to fall. Ghost Boy and POPS ran toward the source of the RF radiation, the command center.

Sergeant Johansen and another Marine destroyed the sonic emitter and began targeting the parabolic antennas. When or by whom it was discovered that the drones were no longer protected by the shield system was not clear but it was immediately apparent that they were as vulnerable as they had appeared invincible a moment before. Within minutes the atomic army crumbled.

### ∴∴∴

Joyce Cummins was discovered in the command center cradling Gayle Henderson's lifeless body and rolling a cyanide capsule around in her mouth. In the end he'd taken the easy way out, knowing full well that for all her grit Joyce was unable to do the same. He'd wooed her through her lust to rise above the glass ceiling, and they'd gone after Lynch who Adam Rose had elevated to chief financial officer. A sure check on the purse strings to ensure the safety of a simple man's multi-million dollar company. In the end ambition and envy were Gayle Henderson's undoing.

*THE END*

# FUN TIMES

*I* had a lot of fun writing this story and I hope that it shows through in the storytelling. When I got the Outline for the premise of the series a number of ideas began to percolate. Things that emerged all had the central idea that the setting was a World of Tomorrow sort of time where the values and manners of yesteryear were just as important as art deco styled futuristic technology.

There is for me something very special in the old Science Fiction movies, the ever so serious yet tongue in cheek spirit. Treasure hunters, Rocket Men, and the dastardly Ming, heroes who could stand tall and be gentlemen as well as fierce fighters. So I thought the nice guy hero might work well against seemingly insurmountable odds... I hope you enjoyed Rise of The Atomic Army.

⋮⋮

**J. WALT LAYNE** - lives in Springfield, Ohio. He is a veteran of the US Army, a married father of three, and a voracious reader. A prolific writer, he is the author of Frank Testimony a legal thriller set in Bedford, Mississippi in the 1950s. He is also the author and creator of The Champion City Series of pulp detective stories to be published exclusively by Pro Se Press (March 2013). He has written a laundry list of articles for Backwoodsman Magazine and is the former Op-Ed columnist for The Albany Journal (Albany, Georgia). Watch for numerous short stories from Airship 27 Productions You can catch up with him on Facebook as Author J Walt Layne.

# MONSTER FROM A NIGHTMARE WORLD

## BY ERIK FRANKLIN

**A**lex Conroy sat at his metal desk in the laboratory, doing his utmost to exceed the limits of his powers. The young man fixed his blue eyes unblinkingly on a nearby table, trying to move the piece of furniture across the room. Up until now, his only success was moving small objects with telepathy, and he was determined to increase his power. After all, being the assistant director of S.O.S. (Scientific Operational Security), he had to be ready for action at a moment's notice. "If you rest, you rust!" General Jack Monroe would tell him whenever he was not training. Alex heard the General's words echoing in his mind as he made one last desperate mental effort to shift the table's position.

No such luck. The table remained motionless while Alex slumped on his desk. Using telekinesis was an exhausting feat for him. As he caught his breath he heard heavy footsteps coming towards him. It was the sound of metal hitting the tiled floor, and he knew instantly who it was.

"Are you feeling tired, Alex?" a monotone electronic voice inquired. Alex turned around in his seat to face POPS, and tilted his head to look at the eight foot tall blue robot. The overhead laboratory lights gleamed off of the robot's polished surface as his red optical receptors met Alex's eyes. Though his face was metal and immobile, Alex imagined that he saw a concerned expression.

"It's no use," groaned Alex, nodding towards the table "I can't get the thing to budge."

"I believe the expression is: If at first you do not succeed… try, try again." POPS recited supportingly.

"Yeah, yeah I know…" Alex said as he walked around the table. The laboratory was his fathers' and Alex inherited the space after his murder. He was reluctant to work there at first, since it was a constant reminder of the tragedy, but practicality ruled out. It was one of the most sophisticated labs in North America. Alex Conroy, with his amazing intellect, required nothing less to be an effective assistant director of the S.O.S. He looked around at the various calculations he had scribbled on the many chalkboards in the room. He looked at the sleek, metal furnishings that were tinted various shades of green, blue, and purple due to the lights cast by chemical reactions taking place in test tubes around him. The staff would refer to him by his codename of "Ghost Boy", "genius" or "whiz kid". He could not help but wonder if he deserved the titles at all.

"Hey, POPS?"

"Yes? Is there anything I can help you with?" the robot queried.

"I need to know more about Pronux than just the obvious facts."

POPS stood silently for a moment, accessing his memory banks. It recited the information it knew about the alien being.

"Pronux: humanoid alien, male. Occupation: scientist. Deceased. Most likely the source of your powers..." POPS mechanically read the file aloud then paused "My apologies, I have just given you the obvious facts."

Alex smiled briefly then sighed "I just can't help but wonder... what would I be like if he hadn't entered my life?"

"I imagine much the same, Alex."

"How? Pronux gave me my intellect, not to mention the power to levitate, read minds, become invisible, and use telepathy! My life would be completely different if it weren't for him. Look at all of this work; this is because of Pronux, not Alex Conroy!"

"Abilities aside, Pronux did not give you your courage, loyalty, bravery, patriotism, and cunning." POPS replied firmly. Alex knew that his father had programmed the robot with his knowledge and intellect so he could be the father Alex no longer had, but sometimes he could not shake the feeling that his father's personality was hidden in POPS' circuits as well. Alex could not help but smile.

"If everyone from Pronux's world had these abilities," said Alex as he pointed to the complex formulas on the chalkboard "it must have been an amazing place, before..." he caught himself, remembering the fate that had fallen on Pronux's world.

"Before the nuclear holocaust?"

"Yes, exactly. But can you just imagine a world where everyone had Pronux's genius and abilities?"

"Hypothetically, it would be a wondrous place. However, this is laboring under the assumption that all men were like Pronux. Much like our own world, there would logically be men who would abuse such power for personal gain."

Alex nodded, feeling in his heart that POPS was right.

"I do not mean to discourage any fantasies you have about Pronux's world. It may have been marvelous, but sadly we shall never know. I can only imagine that if Pronux had fled from his world, whatever it was has now become a nightmare world."

"I'll bet. I can't help but wonder…"

Miles away from Alex, scientists were working on the answer to that very question. To the untrained eye it seemed like an abandoned building in the middle of the Arizona desert. A large, three story, grey, flat structure built during World War II that was now obsolete, deteriorating and deserted. Tumbleweeds clung to the chain-link fences while layers of dust blanketed the façade. It was miles off the main road, and held no appeal for any tourists or travelers. It was the perfect place to conceal top secret experiments!

However, it was no longer under S.O.S. control! Under the watchful eye of General Gokor Grinkovitch, the facility was now operating under Soviet control. Grinkovitch, a stocky, hardened Russian veteran of World War II, walked along the catwalk while he watched American scientists set up equipment and prepare for the operation that would define his career and secure his place in history. Occasionally one of the doctors would shoot him a resentful, defiant glare, but that only made Grinkovitch smile. A wave of his hand and one of his soldiers (disguised as American security personal) would shoot them on the spot if he so desired. He took a sip of champagne from the glass he held in his hand. True, it was customary to celebrate with champagne *after* a successful procedure, but he had the utmost confidence in himself. Checking his watch, Grinkovitch saw that they were only minutes away from starting the operation.

"Are we on schedule? We have less than ten minutes!" he growled at the workers.

"Yes, we will be ready!" one of the scientists replied, running last minute checks.

Grinkovitch grunted as he turned away. Another person was approaching him on the catwalk, and he smiled when he saw her. Her name was Adela Drachev, and she was the reason that the Russians were able to infiltrate the base. Drachev's prowess as a spy allowed her to quietly manipulate and undermine the base's security months before the General's arrival, so eventually Grinkovitch could take over. Disguised as a secretary for the S.O.S, she had carefully placed double agents as the security team. Despite being on the eve of success, she had a sour expression on her normally alluring face. Her dark hair fell over her shoulders and onto her firmly crossed arms.

"Agent Drachev, may I offer you a glass of... I forgot, you don't drink." Grinkovitch said as he casually waved his hand away.

"General Grinkovitch, I feel it is not safe for you to be here," she said sternly.

"Relax, Agent Drachev, your cover for me was perfectly conceived! The Americans do not even know they have lost their base! I wish we had equipment like this back in Moscow." He chortled spitefully as he took another sip.

"It is not the deception I am concerned with, General Grinkovitch, it is the experiment. There are too many variables for me to assure your safety."

Grinkovitch waved her off. Even though he was grateful to her, she had been like a mother hen to him ever since he had set foot in enemy territory, and he would not be put off. "As I have been trying to explain to you, Agent Drachev, this is *not* an experiment! From the information our spies have obtained, the Americans have already been successful. We are repeating the results!"

"I have read the same file, and the portal between worlds was not an experiment. It was completely unintentional. Perhaps it was even initiated by the other world, and not the Americans." Drachev insisted. "You don't know if..."

"Just who do you think you are talking to your superior this way? I should have had you court martialed long ago! In any case, our scientists feel that we will be successful, and the American scientists do not have a choice. If they fail, they die! We have replicated the circumstances of that first encounter. Do you dare doubt the finest scientists in Russia as well?" Grinkovitch spat.

Though most would have trembled when Grinkovitch pulled rank on them, Drachev betrayed no sign of emotion, except for her annoyance at the General. Her eyes showed a cold, dead intensity. "General, while you are here, my assignment is to protect you and maintain the illusion that this is still an American base. I cannot guarantee your safety during the experiment..."

"Silence! That is enough from you!" he snapped at her. He pointed a meaty finger towards the head of the American scientists. "Are we ready to begin?"

The American scientist hesitated before answering. He felt the barrel of a rifle press against his back. He turned to see one the "security" officers giving him a threatening look. The scientist tried to think of something to delay the operation, but realized that he could not put off the General any longer. "Yes, sir. We are ready to begin… God forgive us."

Grinkovitch ignored the scientist's lamentation. "Good! Begin the operation!"

The room was silent as the machinery hummed to life. Buttons and control panels lit up like the night sky. The entire room began to gently shake and vibrate while Grinkovitch looked on, his heart pounding in his chest.

"Now!" the General yelled "Get the soldier!"

Moments later, a tall, muscular Russian soldier strode across the laboratory towards the center of the room. His expression was serene, like he was expecting to receive a gift from the gods. Drachev focused on the solider, her anxiety intensifying. She turned to Grinkovitch to express her opinion, but he was a million miles away. His eyes sparkled as he imagined the fame and glory that awaited him back in the motherland.

"Once the operation is completed, we will have our own Ghost Boy! No, a Ghost Man!" he said aloud, though he was really talking to himself. "I will be head of the army with him at my command! Together, with a unit of Ghost Men, we will finally defeat the capitalists and…" Grinkovitch stopped himself. His eyes went even wider as he witnessed the spectacle unfolding beneath him.

A globe of light materialized before the brawny Russian soldier. All eyes were fixed on the beautiful sphere as its radiance illuminated the laboratory. The air crackled with electric energy while it gently pulsed as it increased in size, eventually becoming two stories high. All were mesmerized but Drachev.

"I am concerned, General. The size of the energy field is much larger than the initial one reported by the Americans."

"Will you shut up! This is my moment of triumph!" Grinkovitch said as he shoved her away. Drachev quickly regained her balance and gave her superior an icy glare.

"Now! Go into the portal soldier! You will be reborn a hero!" Grinkovitch pointed towards the globe. The soldier looked up at him and nodded.

As he took steps towards the portal, the soldier could not shake the feeling that he heard a strange noise coming from within the globe. The confidence in his stride faltered as he turned his head to listen closer. There was a noise! It sounded like the breathing of a large, powerful animal. The soldier felt a chill run down his spine.

"There is something alive in there General Grinkovitch!" the soldier turned back to him, shouting. "I can hear it breathing and moving in there! What should I do, sir?"

"It's responding just like the American experiment...a dignitary from the other world is going to grant us power!" Grinkovitch said breathlessly "Do not just stand there, soldier! Take his power now!"

The soldier nodded and cautiously advanced towards the portal. His every instinct was telling him to back away, but he could not ignore the General's command. All eyes were on him, waiting for an alien being to emerge and bestow him with superhuman abilities.

The soldier was the first victim of the terrifying monster that emerged from the glowing orb.

General Jack Monroe poured over the reports that lay spread across his handsome walnut finished wooden desk. His battle-hardened face scrunched up as his eyes shifted from paragraph to paragraph. He heard the door open as Alex walked in the office. The two quickly exchanged salutes while Monroe began to light up one of his trademark reeking cigars, much to the displeasure of Alex. Even though he thought it would be rude to read the General's mind, Alex wondered if Monroe purposefully lit up whenever he was near.

"You wish to see me, sir?" Alex asked.

"I know you and POPS are better with patterns than I am. I want you to go over these reports and let me know what you think." Monroe said as he shifted the papers together into a stack and handed them to Alex. Monroe continued his briefing as Alex began to skim through the pages. "These are communications between our base and another top secret S.O.S. laboratory about fifty miles from here. It was built during the war and has been operating in secret ever since."

"What's the problem?" Alex asked as he examined another teletype letter. So far he was unable to see anything out of the ordinary with their transmissions. They were plainly written data sheets and updates, not unlike what he remembered his parents sending out to their colleagues at the S.O.S.

"That's just it; I can't put my finger on it." Monroe said as he stood up from behind his desk and paced around his office. He looked absentmindedly at the World War II pictures of his old squad hanging on the wall. He paused over one that showed him near a group of Nazi scientists, escorting them to prison. "I can't tell you why, but those communications don't read right to me. I don't know if I'm tired or what, but there is just something about them that's been bothering me for a while."

"They matched all the security codes and got through the scramblers," Alex said as he went over another note, but then he began to see what Monroe was talking about. It was the wording in the letters. Although there was nothing wrong with them at first glance, once Alex studied them more closely he noticed that the reports subtly became stiff, formal, and ultimately vague. As he continued to scan through the documents, Alex saw that the reports began to sound repetitive. He looked up at Monroe, who was nodding grimly.

"Now you see what I mean. I can't prove it, but I'm sure there is something wrong at that base! I want you to investigate, unofficially of course. It's not far from here, and you're going on the pretense of an inspection. If there's nothing wrong then it will be between you and me, and none will be the wiser."

"You got it, sir! POPS and I..." Alex began enthusiastically, but Monroe raised a hand to stop him.

"About that... POPS is going to remain here."

"What? Sir, I need him! He's always goes with me in the field!"

"Yes, but I need him here and I'll show you why."

Monroe reached into his desk and pulled out a pair of glasses. They were black and thick rimmed, and the General handed them to Alex. He tried them on, but found no difference in his vision.

"What are these?" Alex said as he examined the glasses curiously.

"To all appearances these are ordinary spectacles. But the S.O.S. has been developing these babies for the CIA. These little beauties contain a microtrasmitter, a microphone, and a microcamera hidden inside," indicating that the camera was hidden in the bridge of the glasses.

"I see, so you're going to have me wear these while I investigate the laboratory, and POPS will be picking up the transmissions while you watch on the televisor, right?"

"You're too darn smart, kid." Monroe said as he put out his cigar in the ashtray. "Now keep in mind that this is a field test for this gizmo, so you'd better keep them on the whole time."

"Yes, sir," Alex said putting them back on. Monroe got up and opened the door.

"Now I'll be monitoring the situation with POPS, you get a move on!"

Alex had taken a jeep from the base and drove through the Arizona desert to the spot marked on the map. According to Monroe, the glasses were in perfect working order since POPS had seen every minute of the journey. Special wires connected the robot to a viewing screen and Monroe was able to watch the drive via a black and white flickering image. Alex had stopped outside of the supposedly abandoned laboratory. There were no windows and the entire area looked devoid of life. Alex picked up the radio.

"I don't see anyone here. The whole place looks abandoned."

"That's the idea. Now go inside and check it out. You remember the password, right?" Monroe said over the radio.

"Of course!"

Instinctively, Alex scanned the area using telepathy. He did not pick up any signals, nor did he hear the static associated with special agents who could block his skills. The eerie, ever present wind of the desert made Alex feel suddenly alone, as if he was the last man on earth. He spoke into the jeep's radio.

"Sir, there's nobody here! I just scanned the area and didn't pick up a thing! General, I'm going to sneak inside. I'll have to keep silent for a while."

"Right, watch yourself kid." Monroe said, feeling himself grow tense.

Alex got out of the jeep. His apprehension increasing as he drew closer, Alex decided to make himself invisible. He held up his hand and watched the light rays bend around it, turning his entire body transparent. Ghost Boy was needed here.

Ghost Boy looked down and saw that he was leaving footprints in the sand. He thought he would minimize his chance of detection by floating. The invisible genius floated to the door, noticing that it was ajar. Gently pushing it in, he was startled by what he saw!

An armed guard was on the ground, dead. Ghost Boy veered away from the corpse.

"Holy smokes! Are you getting this, sir?"

Startled, Monroe jumped in his seat, and immediately barked at POPS "What do you make of that?"

"Male, deceased. Estimated to be twenty eight to thirty three years of age. United States Army. White streaks in hair indicate loss of pigment, possibly due to fear." The electronic monotone of POPS voice responded.

"Fear?" repeated Monroe in disbelief. He watched as Ghost Boy picked up the dead man's rifle and examine it.

"Every shot's been fired…" Monroe observed.

"That is correct, General." POPS stated "I cannot see any superficial wounds."

Leaving the scene, Ghost Boy floated down a dimly lit corridor and immediately saw carnage in his wake. Large chunks of concrete and debris littered the floor while sparks flew from exposed wires. It was as if a tornado had torn the facility to pieces.

"Holy smokes!" Ghost Boy said under his breath as he advanced. The wreckage reminded him of the story his father had related about Pronux's devastated home world. Despite his shock and awe, Ghost Boy had to remain focused and determine the cause of this catastrophe. He moved further into the lab and spotted another body. He bent down to get a closer look at the man.

"Hey, POPS, you got anything on this guy?" Monroe demanded.

After a few moments of analyzing the image, POPS reported "General Gokor Grinkovitch. Born December 21$^{st}$, 1912. Russian military, currently head of the Advanced Weapons Exploration Unit."

"Well it looks like they need a replacement." Monroe grimly quipped. "If the head of an experimental weapons unit is using this lab… I hate to think what they've been working on… and how the hell did they get in here in the first place?" he shuddered, his face turning crimson.

Ghost Boy looked in the main area of the laboratory, where he surmised that the chaos originated. The lifeless bodies of scientists and soldiers were mixed with the rubble, and Ghost Boy felt sick to his stomach. A large, gaping hole in the concrete wall opposite him caught his attention. Based on the shape of the rubble pattern, something had burst *out* of the room. He performed one more wide scan with his mind, trying to find any witnesses to the event. Nothing came to him, and he decided to relax. Ghost Boy became visible and touched his feet to the ground once more. Gently turning over pieces of concrete and metal, he looked for any clue.

Monroe meanwhile, was growing frustrated.

"Well, maybe it was some kind of explosion from a blasted experiment gone awry!" he ventured without conviction.

"That would not account for the evidence of fear from the first victim Ghost Boy found." POPS countered.

"Well not everyone can take a tank blast like you can!" Monroe snapped "I'd jump out of my boots if I saw a fireball coming at me!"

"That does not account for the lack of scorch marks on the body or his surroundings."

"Oh, well that's…" Monroe began with no idea how he was going to finish the sentence.

"Nor the fact that the soldier fired every bullet he had, yet there are no signs of blood anywhere."

"Well, what's your theory then, metalhead?" Monroe said, folding his arms as he glared at the machine. POPS remained silent for a moment before he replied.

"Insufficient data for a conclusion."

"Can't you just say "I don't know" like the rest of us?" the General grumbled as he continued to watch the screen.

Then, without warning, a gunshot caught everyone off guard! Ghost Boy felt it whiz past his temple as it buried itself into the wall next to him. Reacting on instinct, Ghost Boy became invisible as he dove for cover! Amazingly, another shot rang out and struck only a few inches away from Ghost Boy's hand. He remained still as he looked around frantically. How could anyone see him when he was invisible?

Ghost Boy caught the gleam of a gun barrel aimed straight at him! In a panic, he had unwittingly dived into a corner, and there was no place left to hide! His invisibility was now apparently useless, draining power from his other abilities. He became visible again with one trick left up his sleeve...

The shooter pulled the trigger, but the bullet did not leave the barrel! It gave Ghost Boy the opportunity he needed. Ghost Boy eyed the sniper on the catwalk above him. He ascended quickly to the catwalk, facing the would-be assassin, who was furiously trying to adjust their aim at Ghost Boy's heart. The assassin squeezed the trigger and again, the bullet remained frozen.

Ghost Boy closed the distance between them, and swiftly wrenched the gun from the assassin's hands. Expecting a soldier Ghost Boy was surprised to see the strikingly beautiful face of Drachev as she glared at him. Even without her rifle, she was still a deadly weapon! Drachev struck Ghost Boy with a highly trained punch, and he nearly lost consciousness!

"Another blow like that and it's goodbye Ghost Boy!" he thought to himself.

Leaping back, he took the opportunity to study his new opponent. Her black cat suit revealed the figure of a strong, athletic woman. She was reaching for a blade hidden in her boot, but to her great surprise the knife would not budge from its secret compartment.

Ghost Boy seized the opportunity to strike back! In additional to his mental abilities, he was also a skilled fighter, having trained in Judo and Karate. He fired a side kick into her ribs, sending her backwards onto the catwalk. The whole walkway, damaged beyond repair, shook with the

" DRACHEV STRUCK GHOST BOY WITH A HIGHLY TRAINED PUNCH... "

impact. Ghost Boy knew he had to stop the fight quickly. She may be a witness, and there are too many questions that only she could answer! He tried to read her mind in order to anticipate her next attack, but nothing came to him! Before he had come across static when somebody was deliberately trying to block him... but nothing at all?

Drachev sprang at him again! He had only seconds to execute his counter! Noticing that she was the aggressor, Ghost Boy had the idea to use her own force and momentum against her. He quickly pivoted and caught Drachev's arm. Using all his might, he hurled her over his shoulder with a judo throw and sent her crashing down on the catwalk.

That did it! The force of the struggle caused the whole catwalk to collapse, taking the two of them with it! Drachev had tried to stand, but he tackled her and flung both of them off the falling structure. They rolled on the ground as the sound of bending; clashing metal reverberated throughout the room. Landing on top of her, Ghost Boy stayed his fist and looked intensely into her eyes.

"We could do this all day or we could help each other!" he insisted.

"In my country, we have orders to shoot you on sight!" Drachev growled.

"We're not in Russia, comrade." Ghost Boy said, noticing her accent.

Back at the S.O.S. laboratory, Monroe's mouth dropped as the image of the beautiful spy filled the view screen. POPS observed his reaction.

"She is not in my database of enemy agents. Is something the matter, General?"

"POPS, for once I know something you don't know... that girl is dead!"

"Many spies have faked their deaths in order to execute further operations without suspicion." POPS explained.

"No, you don't understand... she was a Russian agent back in World War II. The Nazis caught her and executed her. I was part of a team that liberated the P.O.W. Camp and found her body... I saw her dead body!"

"Who is she?"

"The Russian officers told me that her name was Adela Drachev... but how is she still alive and looking exactly the same as when I saw her? It's impossible, I tell you!" Monroe shouted.

"As the lone survivor, it is a logical assumption that the Russian agent destroyed the base." POPS surmised.

"I don't think so; my gut's telling me that she's only part of the bigger picture." Monroe said as he lit another cigar. "Let's see what Ghost Boy finds out."

The screen started to falter and flicker, before a static signal replaced the image. POPS began to run a diagnostic function while Monroe spat out his cigar in anger.

"What in Sam Hill is going on? Get the picture back up!"

"The microtransmitter in the spectacles seems to have been damaged in the fight. I cannot re-establish a connection with Alex."

"Let's hope that kid knows what he's doing, because back in WWII, Drachev was as deadly as they come!" Monroe said, his angst growing. Though he would never admit it to Alex, he had grown fond of him, and the thought of anything happening to him made the General's blood boil. He needed to be sure that this was indeed the real Drachev. He needed to see her face to face.

Alex had noticed the crack in his spy glasses and figured they were useless in their current condition, so he pocketed them. Drachev had dusted herself off and Alex was able to dissuade her from fighting. They had gone to neutral corners as Alex learned of the covert Russian takeover of the laboratory. They needed the sophisticated equipment for their operation.

"So you sent those falsified reports..." he surmised. "Then what happened?"

"Grinkovitch was obsessed with his idea to create an army of men like you, Ghost Boy, in order for Russia to take over the world. He was precise with every detail... the *exact* circumstances of the alien Pronux's arrival was recreated. Instead of using a pregnant woman, Grinkovitch recruited a top-notch soldier from our special forces. The soldier was to be the first of many... before the operation took a horrific turn... something emerged from the portal... I cannot quite explain what it was. It was a gigantic creature! It killed everyone and escaped. I was starting to come around when I detected your presence."

Alex pondered the implications of her story. Logically, the monster had come from the same world as Pronux. If Pronux's world contained creatures such as these, beasts either strong enough to endure the nuclear holocaust or mutated by the radiation... then it was truly the nightmare world that POPS had surmised.

Alex was growing more suspicious of Drachev. This woman had tried to kill him and was now suddenly cooperating. Had he convinced her of the futility of battle, or was she trying to play him? He thought the best course of action would be to keep his guard up while he tried to uncover more.

"So how did you survive?" Alex asked, making it a point to keep a suspicious edge in his voice.

"I am a spy, Mr. Conroy, I hid in the shadows after Grinkovitch was killed. The creature had not seen me. A piece of rubble must have struck me on the head, for I remember nothing else after that."

He looked at her, but could not see any discernible signs of injury. Alex felt that a nasty bruise would be developing on his face soon, courtesy of the Russian spy. He knew that various painful bumps would show on his body around the same time... but Drachev, other than looking dirty and disheveled, seemed unharmed.

"And why are you telling me all of this?" he said cagily.

Drachev paused and thought through her response. "Because that creature I saw could destroy the earth... and no doubt your government would wish it destroyed as well. I am assuming that the enemy of my enemy is my friend, no?"

"I can't imagine that Moscow would be too upset with a monster destroying the United States."

"That creature murdered Russians and Americans alike when it came into our world. I am asking for your help, Mr. Conroy, we must destroy the monster!"

Alex nodded. He was unable to read her mind, yet he sensed that she was telling the truth. No doubt Monroe would be flabbergasted at the idea of Ghost Boy teaming up a Russian spy, but if what she was saying turned out to be true, then they had bigger problems on their hands.

"The beast should be fairly easy to track..." Drachev indicated. Alex peered out of the massive hole and saw footprints in the desert sand. Each step (and there were a great many) stretched in a long line, resembling the prints of a massive centipede.

"Holy smokes! How big is this thing?" Alex said in disbelief.

"You shall see for yourself soon enough."

"I kinda hope not..." Alex remarked as he led Drachev out of the ruined laboratory and back to the jeep. Drachev took his arm and stopped him before they climbed in. He was surprised by the strength of her grip.

"Mr. Conroy, do you trust me?" she demanded.

"Huh?" Alex was surprised.

"I asked if you trust me. If we are going to be partners, however temporary, then I need to know that you trust me. I feel that I can trust you."

"Oh well, as you said, enemy of my enemy and all that. But something bothers me about you..."

"And what would that be, Mr. Conrad?"

"Well... how did you know where I was when I was invisible?" It was true that many things bothered him about Drachev, but he thought it best not to mention that he was unable to read her mind. It was better to have her think he could, because if there was one thing that Monroe had taught him... never show weakness to your enemy.

"A simple deduction and educated guess based on the environment and your limited experience in combat. It is what an amateur soldier would do in a combat situation." Drachev answered curtly.

"Limited combat experience! I should have you know..."

"We know of your adventures in Moscow. Your invisibility, your levitation, your..." Drachev dismissively stated. Then a thought occurred to her, and she bent down to pull the knife from her boot. It slid out smoothly and she stared at the blade in disbelief.

"And perhaps, Mr. Conroy, you can explain to me why guns jam when you are near and that I cannot use my knife in your presence. Maybe you have the power to render weapons useless as well?" Drachev asked, with genuine curiosity.

"Perhaps I do..." Alex said, enjoying for the moment that he had outsmarted her. It was a simple matter for him to disarm Drachev: he had used his telekinetic abilities to keep the firing mechanism of the gun in place. When she had reached for her knife, he had used his powers to push the knife back into its sheath. Alex was suddenly thankful for the mental workout that he had put himself through earlier that morning.

He reached for the radio which earned him a suspicious scowl from Drachev. "What are you doing?"

"I'm arranging for some members of the S.O.S. to meet up with us. If that monster destroyed the entire lab, then we're going to need some help taking it on!" Alex replied as he adjusted the frequency.

"I doubt more soldiers will help. You will be throwing away their lives."

He did not answer her as he placed a call to POPS.

Miles away from Alex and Drachev, a military transport truck sped along the bumpy desert road. A U.S. Army driver (who was told to forget everything he saw or heard), listened to the rantings of General Jack Monroe. It had begun with the conditions of the road, then the heat of the desert, and finally, to the issue at hand.

"First a Russian spy comes back from the dead and now our resident genius actually *believes* her story about a blasted monster wrecking the entire lab! This whole thing is too far-fetched to believe!" Monroe snarled as their journey continued.

POPS, who was lying down in the back of the truck, raised his electronic voice to compensate for the noise of the road.

"Considering the events that we have faced, General, one would make the supposition that you would be more open-minded to the unknown." The truck bounced, shaking the large robot. He felt his metal hide for dents or scratches. "Driver, can you please watch the holes?"

"Quit your complaining! I'm tired of being the voice of reason here." Monroe snapped at POPS, even though the robot was not the source of his frustration. He thought of Alex with that Russian agent, and was afraid for him. When Alex contacted Monroe on the radio, he had breathed a sigh of relief. Now, using POPS, they were following Alex's radio signal. Monroe's biggest fear was that Drachev would find a way to manipulate Alex and... no... she could never turn him. Alex Conroy was many things, but he would never betray his country. Most likely, she would try to kill him once she had earned his trust.

"General, I am picking up something unusual." POPS said as he sat up, the top of his head bumping repeatedly against the roof of the transport truck.

"What is it?" Monroe said, snapping out of it.

"I am picking up a radio signal of unknown origin, most likely local, though its location is being scrambled. I cannot tell what is receiving the broadcast." POPS responded.

"It's probably some nearby radio station or something like that. Well, try and trace the damn thing. Maybe the "monster" emits radio waves or something like that." Monroe said dismissively.

"Highly improbable, sir. Biological creatures do not emit sound frequencies that replicate electronic radio signals..."

"Yeah, yeah, I get the picture. Just keep on searching." Monroe said as he lit up another cigar. He caught the driver looking back at the robot with a child-like wonder.

"Keep your blasted eyes on the road, son!"

The driver snapped to attention, but could not resist grinning.

"I'm sorry, sir. It's just that I am a huge fan of science fiction stories and movies... and that robot is out of this world!" The driver said his enthusiasm overflowing.

"I am afraid to disappoint you soldier, but I am of terrestrial origin, built by a human." POPS replied. Monroe could not help but scoff. POPS was programmed to include Dr. Dave Conroy's massive intellect, but the great scientist never bothered with modern slang or expressions.

"What's your name, driver?" Monroe asked.

"Adams, sir. Private Thomas Adams."

Adams was a man who possessed a perpetual smile. He looked to be in his thirties, well groomed, and destined for military success. It was then Monroe noticed that Private Adams had a scar running down the left side of his face. It was in sharp contrast to his youthful appearance.

"Where'd you get the scar, Private?"

"In the war, sir."

"Korea?"

"Yes, sir."

Monroe eyed him with suspicion. He knew that he had never met the man in his life, yet something about him seemed oddly familiar. As Monroe was mentally trying to place him, he noticed Adams looking back at POPS again.

"Well, Private Thomas Adams, if you admire that bucket of bolts so much, then I suggest you keep this damn truck on the road before you bust the thing into a million pieces!" Monroe said. Adams focused his attention back on his driving, his smile completely vanished.

"Do not worry, Private Adams. I assure you that if this vehicle were to crash, I would survive. I am able to withstand a direct tank blast." POPS assured the young man.

"That's incredible!" Adams replied, regaining his sense of wonder.

"I'll get you his damned autograph once we finish this wild goose chase!" Monroe snapped, needed the quiet to think.

"Alex to POPS, Alex to POPS, can you hear me?" Alex's voice came over the radio. The boy sounded determined yet somehow frightened.

"General, I am receiving a transmission from Alex. I will broadcast it." POPS said.

Adams turned excitedly to face Monroe. "Do I get to meet Ghost Boy today too?"

"Shut up, kid!" Monroe said as he waited for Alex to continue his broadcast.

Alex's drive with Drachev had been tense. She was not one for polite conversation, and every attempt that Alex made was met with either short responses, shrugs or silence. Despite their promise of alliance, both could sense a mutual distrust of each other. He would occasionally sneak a glance at her from the passenger side mirror. The sun was beginning to set and amber light was bathing the side of her face. Her eyes, though perceptive and calculating, seemed cold and dead. Drachev would glance over at from time to time and he would pretend that he did not notice.

Periodically, she would ask him one thing: "Anything?"

"No, sorry, I'll keep trying." was all he could offer for the majority of the ride. He had been sending out telepathic signals, doing his best to read the mind of anyone nearby. Alex was able to locate and lock onto several people on the road, but none of them had any thoughts about seeing a monster.

"The footsteps are still going in a straight line. How fast can this thing go?" Alex said aghast.

"I do not know. I only witnessed its attack on the soldiers and scientists." Drachev answered.

"It was a rhetorical question. But anyway, this thing can withstand bullets, right?"

"It did not appear to be harmed by your weapons." Drachev calmly said. She would take every opportunity to indicate when she felt that an American product was inferior. Alex had decided to live with these snide comments, figuring that they would not be partners for much longer.

Suddenly a thought came to Alex. A voice, panicked, almost hysterical.

"*Oh my god! That thing's going to kill me! I have to get out of here! Someone help me!*" A man said to himself.

"*What is it? Does it see me? I can't believe it's real!*" a woman's thoughts.

"*It must be an alien! We're under attack!*" a child's inner voice.

"*A monster! Run for it! Run for it!*" another man's thoughts almost screamed.

Alex grabbed the radio and called out to POPS "Alex to POPS, Alex to POPS, can you hear me?"

"What is it?" Drachev said, sitting up in her seat.

"Go ahead, kid. You got something?" Monroe's voice came over the radio.

"I just heard several people thinking. A monster is attacking them! They sounded terrified possibly trapped, General! Are there any towns or cities nearby?"

"I have located a town named Gordon Flats not far from your position. Established in 1910. Current population: 600. Keep your present direction and it should be within visual range momentarily." POPS replied.

"I'll bet that's where the thing is. Alright S.O.S., let's meet up at Gordon Flats and stop this monster!" Alex yelled.

"I doubt it will be as easy as all that." Drachev said bitterly under her breath.

"Is that Ghost Boy?" Adams said.

"Yes, and I'll get you his damned autograph too if you get us Gordon Flats pronto without crashing this blasted truck!" Monroe yelled.

Alex pressed the pedal down as far as it could go and the two sped through the desert at a rapid pace, flying over the hills. Drachev was getting tense, gearing herself up for a fight. Alex looked to her and thought that it would be best to take her lead. After all, she had seen the monster firsthand and admittedly had more field combat experience than he did.

As they got closer, more frightened thoughts from the citizens of Gordon Flats entered his mind. The panic in their voices made Alex squeeze the steering wheel tighter. He thought of the people from Pronux's world and imagined their screams magnified in the millions. Maybe Pronux had tried to save his people from this very creature and failed. What chance did Alex Conroy have? He could not help but feel responsible, however indirectly, for bringing the monster into the world. If Pronux had never bestowed his powers to him, the Russians could not have imagined that a portal existed.

Another telepathic thought came to him. It was in a distorted, deep voice, and unlike the rest of the people in the Gordon Flats, it was calm and methodical.

*"This is a strange world. These small creatures are different from the ones of my world, yet similarly weak and harmless. The structures on this planet are feeble; they crumble easily with only the slightest effort. Some of the small creatures are trying to harm me again, but I'll tend to them soon. I am too hungry to focus; the sand does not provide the energy that my home world feeds me... but this brown blood may sate my appetite until I can find it!"*

Alex was stunned. He had heard the voice of the monster. Suddenly another thought reached Alex's mind.

*"That thing just knocked over the gas pumps! My god, it's drinking the gasoline!"*

Alex assumed that the creature was a mindless beast, driven by the same primal instincts that governed most living creatures. Alex realized the creature, though not able to express itself verbally, was cunning, intelligent and more deadly than he had imagined.

"...THE TWO SPED THROUGH THE DESERT AT A RAPID PACE..."

"Oh my god, I can hear it!" Alex exclaimed "I can actually hear what it is thinking!"

"That should help us plan an attack against it... look!" Drachev said, pointing towards the horizon. Alex could not see anything at first except for the silhouette of Gordon Flats. It looked to be a small, but growing city built in the middle of the desert. The largest building was only three stories tall and the architecture of the town was mainly composed of brick and mortar. Some neon signs had been turned on; glowing brightly against the setting sun, but Alex could see no signs of anything unusual.

"I don't see anything, Agent Drachev." Alex admitted.

"Look over there, you will see it!" she pointed.

She was correct. As they got closer to the town, Ghost Boy spotted the monster! The shadowy outline of a beast was visible against the sunset of the city, with more details becoming clearer as they got closer. Ghost Boy guessed that the creature was about twenty feet tall and resembled some mutated form of insect. The colossal beast possessed massively long forearms similar to those of a praying mantis, with the long body of a centipede and the armor plating of a beetle. Ant-like pincers were located on the corners of its mouth, the eyes were of a mantis, but it lacked antenna. Its coloration was iridescent, and its armored plating revealed the scars of many battles. It emitted a strange cry that was similar to the voice Ghost Boy heard in his head: deep and distorted. Maybe he imagined it, but Ghost Boy swore that the monster's voice was inherently evil. It moved with supreme confidence as it terrorized the citizens, enjoying every minute.

"Holy smokes!" gasped Ghost Boy "It's even larger than I imagined but that's not possible! Clearly, according to the theory of gigantism, earth's gravity could not support the support the monster's bone structure and..."

"And it's here now, ignoring your theory. What are we going to do about it!" Drachev replied.

Its forearms tore apart another gas pump with ease, like a child knocking around wooden blocks. The creature craned its head over the gas geyser which erupted from the ground, positioning itself so the brown liquid would shoot directly into its mouth.

"*Not as substantial, but it will do. I miss the energy from my world. These creatures are beginning to annoy me. I will rid myself of them before continuing to feed!*" Ghost Boy heard the monster once again as it finished drinking the fountain of gasoline. It turned its massive body around and faced a blockade of police cars. They were positioned, bumper to bumper, to prevent the monster from the entering the remainder of the town.

A squad of police officers were firing at the beast with every possible weapon they could get their hands on! Rifles and shotguns hurled bullets at the creature, but their efforts were in vain. Gunfire bounced off the creature's armor plated exoskeleton as it moved towards the officers. The great insect reached across and crushed one of the police cars with its mantis-like claw, skewering the roof of the vehicle. The men retreated as the monster swept its other arm across the road, sending the police cars flying into storefronts and bouncing down the street. The officers ducked behind buildings and windows. They kept firing valiantly at the monster, but their efforts were futile.

"Since you haven't mention it yet, Agent Drachev... exactly what is your plan to stop this thing?" Ghost Boy said as their jeep reached the outskirts of town. They got out and ran down Main Street through a crowd of terrified people, towards the monster.

"I have no plan as yet. All I know is that with your abilities you have a better chance than your police force." Drachev said as she checked her sniper rifle again. "At the very least, you know what it is thinking."

"So... no plan then..." Ghost Boy said, realizing that he must formulate a plan himself.

*"They have been depleted for now. Perhaps while they gather strength I will finish feeding."*

"It's going back for seconds!" Ghost Boy said as the two hid behind a nearby building, the stench of gasoline fumes reaching their noses. "Now, we both need to think of a plan and fast!"

Drachev looked down at her weapon and slung it over her shoulder "Regular bullets are useless, and I do not have the time to readjust and recalibrate my weapon for the use of explosive-tipped bullets. What do you suggest?"

Ghost Boy looked over at the gas station. The creature had yanked another gas pump out of the ground and flung it carelessly through a diner window while it drank from a fountain of gasoline. An idea came to Ghost Boy and he turned to Drachev.

"I heard that thing say "brown blood". It has no idea what gasoline is! Maybe if we can ignite it..." Ghost Boy said.

Drachev thought about the plan and quickly nodded. She looked around hurriedly; the street was now covered in debris and ruins. Amongst the litter she saw a discarded cigarette lighter, most likely fallen out of someone's pocket. Picking it up, she handed it to Ghost Boy.

"Yeah, that'll do." He took it from her. He did not see anyone nearby, nor was he able to read any minds in the vicinity, so Ghost Boy deemed it safe to carry out the plan. Leaning back, Ghost Boy flicked the lighter and threw it as far as he could. Though he had a strong throwing arm, the distance was aided by his telekinesis. The lighter landed in a puddle of gasoline and Drachev nodded, somewhat impressed.

"That was a good throw!" she exclaimed.

"I was the best pitcher on my baseball team when I was a kid," he said "now do your stuff!"

Drachev instantly understood his meaning. Putting the rifle sight to her eyes, she aimed at the small lighter. Ghost Boy never saw anyone with more precise control over their body movements; it was as if she ceased breathing! Drachev squeezed the trigger.

Her bullet sailed through the air and exploded the lighter! The flames from the explosion spread through the gasoline, and a chain reaction transformed the fountain of gasoline into a tower of fire! The monster roared as its jaws were scorched by the flames, throwing its head backwards in agony while flames shot down its throat. Soon the flames spread and the entire gas station was consumed in a massive fireball, engulfing the monster's body in the inferno as well! The ground shook as windows exploded from the sonic force of the blast. Another roar from the creature could be heard over the blast, it sounded as if it was in pain... dying.

Ghost Boy tried to read the monster's thoughts... but nothing came. He looked to Drachev, who was sternly watching the massive cloud of smoke that was blanketing the area.

"You don't suppose that did it, do you?" Ghost Boy asked her uncertainly. "Is it thinking now?"

"It's not thinking anything... it might be dead!" he said optimistically, though a part of him doubted that this was true. It came from a nightmare world that had been destroyed in a nuclear holocaust. If it could survive the radiation, then perhaps this explosion would have caused it pain, but nothing more than that. He was reluctant to move, but Alex decided the only sure way to find out was to walk through the black haze and examine the body.

At that moment they heard a truck screech behind them. Alex looked over to see a very irate General Jack Monroe stomping towards them, accompanied by a naive, eager looking soldier. Private Adams looked at the aftermath in disbelief, his mouth hung low as he gaped.

"A real life robot, Ghost Boy, and a giant monster!" Adams gasped. "This is unbelievable!"

"It'll seem all the more real when we get the bill for the damage you caused to this town!" Monroe rounded on Alex, stammering with anger. "We needed to direct this creature away from people, and the first thing you do is let it run loose while you blow up the town's gas station!"

"I do not think that one can direct this monster, let alone kill it cleanly." Drachev said, stepping up to Monroe in defiance. Alex appreciated the gesture, but noticed the expression on Monroe's face.

The tough, hardened old soldier showed signs of astonishment. His eyes were wide with shock, his cigar in danger of tumbling from his mouth. It was clear that something about her made him stammer.

"Exactly who are you..." Monroe said, deciding to play dumb.

"How dare you speak to me this way! Mr. Conroy and I did the best we could to save this small town." she continued.

"General, this is Adela Drachev. A Russian spy." Alex said, more interested in Monroe's emotional turmoil.

"Wow! Wait... we're working with the Russians now?" Adams asked in disbelief.

Their attention was shifted to the truck beside them as it shifted, sank, and then raised itself up again as POPS emerged from the back. He walked towards the group, scanning the area.

"It seems as if I'm too late to be of any assistance." POPS said to Alex. Suddenly, the robot stopped and looked at Drachev, its optical sensors taking readings from her.

"Fascinating..." POPS said. Drachev gave the robot a fierce look, as if her eyes were commanding him to stop. Monroe looked at POPS, hoping to hear some kind of answer to the mystery of Drachev.

"*IT BURNS! The creatures of this planet are more clever than I first thought! I must get my revenge before I find food! I cannot allow them to hurt me AGAIN!*"

Ghost Boy raised a hand and yelled for everyone to stop. "It's still alive!"

All eyes looked to the smoke cloud as the form of the monster could be seen rising up inside it! The beast shook its head and started crawling towards the small group, the only humans it could find. Monroe and Adams raised their weapons, but Drachev calmly placed her hand on Adams's gun, lowering it.

"Save your bullets. We need something much stronger!"

Ghost Boy looked around for another source of fire, but found nothing. Fearlessly, POPS strode determinedly towards the monster. Despite the robot's towering height and bulk, POPS had to crane its head back to see the eyes of the creature looming over it.

"POPS, get back!" Ghost Boy yelled, "You're no match for it!"

"I'm the most effective weapon that we currently have. I will buy you some time." POPS said as it struck the monster's armored plating with its metal fist. The monster recoiled slightly from the blow, and POPS drove another straight punch into the same spot. Even though the beast's plating could deflect bullets, POPS' mechanized, relentless punches were beginning to crack through its exoskeleton.

But the beast's retaliation was swift and terrible! It brought its giant claw crashing down towards POPS! The robot leapt away at the last second, saving himself from impalement! The claw tore a large hole in the ground where the robot had stood, the tip of its forearm burrowing into the earth. The beast wrenched its appendage free and swiped across the ground with its other claw. POPS only had time to raise its arms in defense as it took the full brunt of the swat! The robot was violently hurled across the street; its fall was broken when POPS crashed into the side of a bus, completely caving in the side.

*"This shining beast almost pierced my skin! I will tear it apart!"*

POPS stood up again, and looked to see the monster beginning to close its arms in a scissor-like motion! POPS ran forward, narrowly avoiding the beast's crushing maneuver, and raised its fists again. The robot valiantly hammered away in the same damaged area it started breaking through earlier.

Ghost Boy looked around, there had to be something he could do to help POPS! Thinking quickly, he spotted a large, brightly lit neon blue sign attached to a bowling alley proudly announcing the name "Husser Bowling Haven." The monster's centipede-like body was writhing underneath the sign. It was obvious the creature was vulnerable to fire... so why not electricity?

Turning himself invisible, Ghost Boy hovered over to the roof of the bowling alley and landed near the sign. After a quick examination of the structure, Ghost Boy began to use his telekinesis to dismantle the supports.

"I may not be strong enough to move something this big," Ghost Boy thought to himself "but these small bolts are a piece of cake! I just hope that POPS can keep this thing still while I work!"

Drachev looked through her sniper rifle, checking on POPS' progress with the creature. It was nearly through the plate of armor, and the monster was furious! It kept trying to jab at the robot, but POPS was able to dodge most of the hits. He was waiting for the perfect moment to strike.

"Timber!" Ghost Boy yelled as the sign snapped off its hinges. It collapsed on the monster's centipede-like body. The creature roared in pain from the impact, bending backwards in agony. The sign began to spark, electrocuting the beast. With that stroke of luck, POPS broke through the armor plating! Soft skin was now visible through the damaged plating. A subtle pulsing beat under the surface of the skin suggested that vital organs were placed there! Though the hole was only the size of POPS' fist, it was now a weak spot that could be exploited.

However, this fight was far from over. An animal is never more deadly than when it has been wounded, and this monster was no exception! In a burst of speed, it seized POPS in its pincers and held it high in the air.

"Holy smokes! POPS!" Ghost Boy yelled, astonished and horrified by what he saw.

"*DIE! DIE! DIE!*" thought the beast as it shook the robot brutally from side to side.

Then monster began slamming POPS violently into the ground! Large chunks of concrete and pavement burst from the street as the robot's body was forced down beneath the pavement. POPS' armor, which could withstand almost anything on earth, was now bent, dented, and breached. The monster held POPS up for examination, and saw that the machine was unmoving. An occasional spark would emit from an exposed circuit, but nothing more.

"POPS..." Ghost Boy said as he floated towards the ground. He had to do something to get POPS free from the monster's grip.

"*While it is weak...destroy the robot! Make it look like an accident! It knows too much!*"

The voice caught Ghost Boy off guard. He was accustomed to hearing the monster's thoughts by now, but he had never heard this voice before. It was human, younger, and it matched...

"What?" Ghost Boy said aloud in surprise. He had to get back to Monroe and warn him!

The loud crack of Drachev's sniper rifle made Monroe jump. He was so focused on POPS that he had forgotten all about the Russian spy. He looked, and to his horror, saw a bullet bounce off POPS's armor! He wheeled around and yanked her gun down.

"What the hell do you think you're doing!"

"I was aiming for the monster's wound but it used the robot to block it!"

"I think it is the other way around! I knew we could never trust a Commie rat!" Monroe said as he seized her weapon and pulled out his pistol, aiming it at her chest. Adams turned to both of them, shocked.

"Sir, what are you doing? The woman missed accidentally!" Adams pleaded.

Monroe fixed her with a knowing expression, for things were starting to become clear to him. "So you just needed us to weaken the beast, huh? You take out our robot, the monster, and maybe even Ghost Boy in one fell swoop? Was that your plan?"

Drachev stood silently, her eyes fixed on Monroe's. "I was given new orders once Grinkovitch's plan had failed..."

"Orders by whom?" he demanded.

"Sir, shouldn't we be trying to fight the monster?" Adams asked, his voice jittering. The beast had discarded POPS and was now crawling towards them. Suddenly, the sound of jet engines filled the sky. The monster looked upwards and roared at the approaching U.S. Air Force Starfighter jets.

"I called in the Air Force, which ought to keep that damned monster busy while we sort this thing out."

The Starfighter jets rained machine gun and rocket fire on the colossal insect. Although it was not greatly affected by the bombardment, it was starting to grow tired. The creature, bored with this town and of the attacks, decided to crawl away. It continued on the straight path out of town, knocking over anything that got in its way as it sought refuge from the Air Force.

On his way to warn Monroe, Alex was stopped by POPS' voice. He had dragged himself across the street to an automotive repair shop and had started to restore his body with the tools from a workbench. Alex rushed over to him and felt a flood of emotion stifle his voice. It pained him to see this robot, the last link that he had with his father, on the verge of death.

"POPS..."

"Do not concern yourself with me, Alex. I dare say that I will pull through, but there is something I must tell you." His electronic monotone sounding normal.

"I need to tell *you* something POPS..." Alex began urgently.

"I have a feeling that our stories will intertwine. Adela Drachev is *not* a human being."

Alex was stunned "Wait... what?"

"Relay that information to General Monroe. Hurry, Alex, time is of the essence!"

Alex reluctantly ran off while POPS continued to repair his transistors.

Monroe held his gun on Drachev. Taking the hint, Adams pointed his rifle at the Russian spy. Monroe looked around at the devastation caused by the monster and shook his head in shame.

"None of this ever needed to happen, Drachev. You damn Commies should have left well enough alone! Now there's something I want to know... why did you try to take out POPS when we still have that monster to contend with?"

"...I was ordered to..." she said haltingly.

"What orders? I never gave you any orders!" Monroe yelled.

"But he did!" shouted Alex.

All eyes turned to Alex as he ran up to Private Adams, yanking the rifle out of his hands and pointing it at his chest. Adams eyes bulged with surprise. Monroe, too, was shocked, but quickly maintained his calm. Drachev stood motionless.

"What... what do you mean? General, do you really believe this? I'm just a private! He's gone crazy." Adams stammered as sweat began to trickle down his brow.

"I tend to go with my gut," said Monroe "and my gut told me to investigate that lab," he pointed his pistol at Adams "and now it's telling me that Ghost Boy is right... you're in on it, along with you, Drachev... or whatever you are."

Adams sighed and shrugged. Alex wanted to pummel him for his betrayal, and for ordering POPS's execution, but they needed to get to the bottom of this. He looked at Drachev and felt a pang of regret. The two were working well together, and they could have made a great team. Had she really been plotting to kill him the entire time?

As if to answer his unspoken thoughts, Adams turned to Alex, "Don't feel too badly about anything, kid. She only does what I tell her to."

"What *you* tell her?" Alex said.

"Yes. You see, agent Drachev has no free will of her own, I've seen to that. She is still the perfect Russian spy, but now incapable of resisting or altering orders. *My* orders, to be precise." Adams said, a smug smile appearing on his face.

"I found her dead body in 1945... how is she still alive?" Monroe demanded.

"Oh she isn't... alive that is. When I was working for the Nazis..." Adams started to explain, clearly enjoying the spotlight.

"Nazis... wait a minute... now I recognize you! It's been eating at me since I laid eyes on you!" Monroe growled, his eyes burning with fury while Adams smiled. "You're that Nazi butcher Wolfgang Schmidt! We hunted you all over the world but nobody was ever able to track you down! You're the..."

"Frankenstein of the Reich, yes. I was able to transform my face for the most part, but despite all my surgical skills, this cursed scar still remains! I do enjoy looking younger." Adams grinned, as he allowed his natural German accent to re-enter his speech. "You see, the reason no one ever found me was that the Russians had recruited me. I was working on an experiment for the Reich. When our soldiers were rapidly dwindling the Fuhrer demanded that we replace them. Well, all the able men of Germany were either already fighting or dead. I experimented and found a way to bring them back. The war ended before I was of any use to the Nazis... but the Russians on the other hand..."

Adams walked over and touched Drachev on the shoulder, as if he were showing off his new sports car.

"You see, I was able to reanimate the dead, and they retained all their muscle memory and skills they had in their previous life... but none of the mental fortitude to make major decisions on their own. That's why..." he tapped her head "I have installed a radio transmitter in her brain. There is an identical transmitter inserted in me. The Russians needed her back, since she was their greatest spy. When they recovered her body, I operated on her, and now she obeys my every order with all the skills she had in her previous life. Of course, she was clever enough to rearrange paperwork that kept me close by. My cover was that of an American soldier, assigned to chauffeur you, General Monroe. "

"So that's why she suddenly suggested we become partners... you told her to! And that's why I couldn't read her mind... she had no thoughts of her own!"

"Correct on both accounts! I followed the orders given to me by the Russian Command  until the monster came into our world. I felt the monster was more threatening than Ghost Boy, and its destruction was my priority. Everything was going well until that cursed robot picked up the radio waves and deduced what she was. I took a gamble and lost." Adams sighed.

While they talked, military vehicles came into the town, surrounding the area. The soldiers reported to Monroe and he issued them orders. "Listen men, these two are Russian spies. I want you to keep them under lock and key!"

"Yes, sir!" a sergeant said as he trained his weapon on Adams. Alex began walking towards POPS when he heard a soldier give a report to the Field Commander.

"Sir, we have a report on that giant monster! The Air Force said it was heading towards the Ravendorf Nuclear Power Plant!"

Alex stopped and he felt the world slow down around him. Nuclear power! That is what the creature was hungry for! Its main food source was the radiation and nuclear waste from Pronux's world! He called over to Monroe, who heard the same report.

"What are we going to do, sir?" Alex asked.

"I told them about the hole POPS punched into it, but I don't think it's wide enough for them to hit! We need a sniper that can hit a target that small with an explosive round..." Monroe grumbled.

It was a long shot, but it was the only plan that Alex could think of. "What about Drachev?"

"What? No Alex, she's under the control of that madman! There's no way that we can get her to cooperate!"

"Let me try. I have an idea!" Alex said, bolting towards Drachev and Adams. The two were sitting together, handcuffed to a bench and guarded by three soldiers. Adams appeared bored as he drummed his fingers, looking more like a man waiting for a bus than for a lifetime of imprisonment. Drachev was sitting still with a stone cold expression. Standing in front of them, Alex spoke only to Drachev.

"Adela, that monster is going to destroy a nuclear power plant, we have to stop it!"

She looked at him, but said nothing. Her eyes were cold, and Adams leaned back against the bench.

"You are talking to the puppet, not the puppeteer. And if an American nuclear reactor is destroyed, I do not care. I doubt my assistance will get me leniency."

"I'm not talking to you, I'm talking to her!" Alex insisted. "Now listen Adela, when you were trying to kill me, it may have been his orders, but it was your instinct that caused you to miss!"

"Impossible, Ghost Boy. She cannot countermand an order."

Alex stared at her. His fierce blue eyes locked onto her dead, green gaze.

"No. No she was able to figure out where I was going, but she somehow missed me. Just like she missed the shot with POPS. Adela is fighting you! She has been this entire time!"

"Nonsense. As you Americans say, you are grasping at straws. She operates only on instinct and muscle memory. There is no decision making, period! Now stop wasting everyone's time and destroy that monster!" Adams shouted in his German accent.

"We need her help!"

"And I want you to guarantee amnesty!" Adams shouted.

"I don't have the authority to do that." Alex said angrily. Even if he could, he would refuse. There had to be some way to get Drachev's help without letting this madman get off Scott free! Adams looked expectantly at him, waiting for him to cave in. Drachev's eyes fluttered, and she turned to Adams with a look of horror and revulsion on her face.

"You... you are a Nazi!"

"Yes..." he snapped, but then he saw the expression in her eyes. A fury whirled within them. It suddenly dawned on Adams that he had lost control of Drachev! She pulled the knife from her boot and swung at him! It was only Ghost Boy's lightning quick reflexes that prevented the Nazi's death. Alex wrestled the blade away from her.

"No, Adela, no! I understand how you must feel, but killing him will not bring justice! He'll face trial for his crimes here!"

Adams, meanwhile, was stunned.

"But what, how? How did I lose control?"

POPS lumbered towards them. He had managed to patch himself up to a functioning condition. The robot looked at Adams and waved a warning finger.

"It was a simple task to isolate your radio frequency and jam it. Agent Drachev is no longer under your control."

"Take him away!" Monroe snapped at the soldiers guarding Adams. They loaded the Nazi scientist in the back of a troop carrier and sped away from the destroyed town. The General faced Alex, Drachev, and POPS.

"The Air Force hasn't been able to make a dent in that blasted creature, and it's still heading for the power plant! The Army's set up a division of tanks located between the plant and the monster, but I doubt they'll be much good. Since it looks like POPS is down for the count, I'm afraid our only option is you two," Monroe pointed at Alex and Drachev "Good luck. The world's counting on you!"

"Is this as fast as this thing can go?" Drachev asked, already knowing the answer.

"Yes, sorry."

" YOU ARE TALKING TO THE PUPPET, NOT THE PUPPETEER. "

"I hate these American vehicles!"

Night had fallen over the desert. Having taken another jeep, Alex and Drachev drove through the desert, hot on the trail of the monster. Its tracks were easy to follow, as was the devastation in its wake. Overturned cars and ruined buildings were accompanied by the scorch marks and explosions from the Air Force's attempt to stop it. Drachev now looked at the wreckage through eyes were no longer dead. They betrayed sadness and confusion, and Alex could not help but comment.

"Are you alright, Adela?" he asked her, genuinely concerned.

"I will not fail you on this mission, if that is what you are asking." she replied sharply.

"No, I'm asking how you feel." Alex said firmly.

"I feel... like you must feel..." Drachev said after thinking a moment "I feel like an abomination."

"How so?"

"I am not natural. There is nothing else on earth like me. I am a monstrosity created by science. I wish to not live again." Drachev said flatly.

Alex was quiet for a moment, but then thought back to what his parents told him. It was true that growing up, he had felt different from the other children, and there were times he cursed his abilities and his life. Alex spoke, but heard his father's voice instead.

"Yes, it is true that you are different from everyone else, but think of the opportunity. You have abilities and talents that far exceed those of anyone else on the planet. You can use your powers to be a tremendous force of good in this world."

"And who decides what is good? Who gives the orders?" she asked him combatively. She did not feel any hostility towards Alex, but the truth was that she was frightened. All of her life she was given orders, and she was comfortable with that. Now that her connection with Adam was severed, she was on her own for the first time since she could remember.

"You could... you could always work for us. The S.O.S. could use someone with your talents." Alex offered.

"No, though I am working with you now, I could never betray my people. Adams was right, we need to stop that monster before it destroys the world. After that, I disappear."

"Where?"

Drachev remained silent and Alex decided to not pursue it. She grabbed her rifle and began to make various adjustments to the weapon. Drachev caught him looking at it.

"It is a weapon of my own design. It can kill a man silently or take out a tank with one bullet if I desire. I am changing it so it will kill the monster."

"How many shots do you have?"

"One."

"One!" Alex said in shock.

"I only carry one on my missions. It is all that I require. You must understand, Mr. Conroy, these explosive rounds are of my design and need extremely specialized materials which are..."

"I get the picture, Adela. I know you're a great shot and all... but I was thinking that we had more to work with!"

"Is the monster nearby?" Drachev said, ignoring Alex's comment.

Alex extended his telepathy, searching the desert ahead of them for signs of the creature's brainwaves. He felt something and reported back to Drachev.

"I'm getting something... not clear words like before. It must be too far away, but I sense something like a... like a primal instinct. The monster is hungry, really hungry!"

Miles away, Colonel Edwards was looking through binoculars at the massive insect heading towards him. The Starfighters from the Air Force had since departed to replenish their missiles. They had depleted their supply while trying to kill the monster.

A row of M103 heavy tanks was positioned in front of Colonel Edwards, with all guns pointing at the beast. His soldiers had already evacuated the facility of all non-essential personnel, and his men were now by his side aiming their weapons at the monster. The officer felt a sinking feeling in his stomach as he thought of the upcoming battle. Nothing anyone had thrown at it was able to stop the monster, and he heard about the destruction it caused at Gordon Flats.

A soldier ran up to him with a handheld radio, they exchanged salutes and the soldier passed it to him.

"General Monroe for you, sir!"

"Thanks," Edwards said as he took the radio "Colonel Edwards here, over."

"Listen Colonel, this is General Jack Monroe of the S.O.S. I've got some agents that are on their way. They have a shot at stopping the monster. Over."

"With all due respect sir, the Air Force wasn't able to stop it, so I doubt a few men are going to be able to do much good! Over." Edwards said, starting to feel agitated.

"They know what they're doing, and I don't want your tanks to start shooting and blow them to pieces before they kill that damned monster! Over!"

"General, I'm the last line of defense before that thing destroys the power plant, and I'm not going to sit here twiddling my thumbs waiting for a miracle! Once it's in range, we're going to blast it to Kingdom Come!" Edwards yelled back, dispensing with formalities.

"Are you countermanding orders from your superior officer? Hold off the attack or I'll see you court martialed so fast your head will spin!"

Before Edwards could answer, another solider ran up to him. "Sir, the tank commanders report that the monster is in range. What are your orders?"

Edwards drowned out the raving voice of General Monroe as he looked from the power plant to the monster. His decision was clear.

"Open fire!" he yelled as he handed the radio back to the soldier. The sounds of Monroe cursing were soon drowned out by the roaring guns of the tanks. The ground shook from the force as shells rained down on the massive insect. Edwards looked through his binoculars and watched as explosions illuminated the monster. It roared in anger, but it pressed on through the assault with fierce determination. The Colonel broke out in a cold sweat and his hands began to shake. Nothing would stop this beast, and he was out of options! He put the binoculars down, stunned.

If he had shifted his binoculars, he would have seen a jeep speeding towards the monster. Ghost Boy watched as the explosions grew closer, and was beginning to get worried as the stray shots were coming nearer to them. He yanked the radio from the jeep and yelled over the explosions.

"Holy smokes! Is there any way you can get them to stop shooting?" Ghost Boy asked Monroe angrily.

"I tried but the damned fool wouldn't hear a word of it! I'm sorry, kid." Monroe replied, the tension and regret in his voice was apparent.

Ghost Boy looked at the oncoming shells and started to swerve the jeep to avoid the explosions. Dirt and sand blasted up from the shell impacts. Ghost Boy and Drachev were surrounded by clouds of sand, doing their best to fight their way to the monster.

"I cannot see in these conditions!" Drachev said as she spat dust out of her mouth. She was trying to look through her sniper scope, but alas could only see gritty brown sand hanging in the air.

"Yeah, it's not that easy driving either!" Ghost Boy snapped back as he turned a hard right, avoiding another explosion that was just feet away!

They were driving towards the front of the creature, and Ghost Boy could hear its thoughts once again.

*"It is so close... and the explosions from these metal creatures keep annoying me!"*

Enraged by the attacks, the monster rose up and flicked its arms out, as if trying to swat away the oncoming shells. As it reared back, Ghost Boy spotted the open wound inflicted by POPS and indicated it to Drachev. She aimed at it, but after a few moments, turned to Ghost Boy with an irritated expression.

"Between the creature's flailing and your driving, I cannot get a clear shot!"

"Well what do you want me to do?" Ghost Boy yelled over the explosions in frustration.

"Either you get your military to stop firing or you get that creature to stop moving!" she demanded.

During the bombardment, Ghost Boy noticed that the tanks had fired almost simultaneously each time. It had helped him in planning a route to avoid their fire, but he was wondering if perhaps this could buy Drachev the time she needed. She aimed at the beast while it shrugged off the tank shells, still moving towards the power plant. The great insect had not noticed them yet, and a hasty plan formed in Ghost Boy's head. It would require strength far greater than he knew he was capable of, but if he had to die in order to save the world, Alex Conroy was prepared to do it. He explained his plan to Drachev as quickly as he could.

Edwards watched as the tanks fired another volley of shells. By this time he did not need binoculars to see the monster. The colossal insect was closing in fast, and the tank commanders were ordering their drivers to steadily retreat. To the great surprise of everyone in the battle zone, the shells were suddenly suspended in midair! Even the monster, which had braced itself for the incoming projectiles, crooked its head in wonder.

*"What? Why are they still? What kind of trick is this?"*

The monster was about to find out! On the ground below, Drachev was finally able to center her aim on the monster's wound. The creature's amazement had caused it to stop moving erratically. Ghost Boy, meanwhile, was straining with all his might as he concentrated on the tank shells. He did not know the consequences of overextending his telekinetic powers, but he felt like his mind was being ripped apart! Feeling pain unlike anything he had ever experienced before, he strained to keep the shells in the air. His neck twitching, he looked over just in time to see Drachev pull the trigger.

Her explosive-tipped bullet rocketed towards the monster. Time seemed to move in slow motion as the bullet sailed through the air. Suddenly, the creature emitted a roar of tremendous agony as it protectively moved its arms to cover its open wound. Drachev had hit the target! A few seconds had passed since the creature was hit, then the monster suddenly jerked in pain. It was the explosive detonating inside its body.

His energy nearly depleted, Ghost Boy let the tank shells drop to the earth. He was sweating profusely, had a pounding, blinding migraine, and was nearly unable to move. By this time Edwards had ordered his men to stop firing as they watched the scene unfold. The massive creature swayed in place, teetering back and forth. The sounds it emitted were low grunts and stifled roars, as if the insect was confused. It tried to extend an arm to brace itself against the sand, but its efforts were in vain. Its arm buckled under the pressure of its own weight and the monster collapsed onto the sand, sending a great wave of dust in the air.

Alex tried to read the thoughts of the creature, but nothing came to him. It seemed that the titanic struggle was over. The monster died within a thousand feet of reaching the power plant. Alex turned to Drachev, whose eyes were fixed on the monster. It took everything he had, but Alex managed to speak.

"I think we make a pretty good team." he said forcing a weak smile.

She turned to him and pointed her rifle at his head. "Even though I am out of explosive rounds, regular bullets still work with my gun." Drachev said as she loaded them. "My orders from my country are clear: kill the Ghost Boy on sight."

"Adela, don't do this... please... you are not a slave to your orders!" he exclaimed faintly. "You have your free will back, Adela... use it!"

"Stop using my first name! To you, I am Agent Drachev!"

"No, to me you are another human being who needs help."

She stood over him, her finger hovering over the trigger. The only sign that his words may be having any impact was the fact that she had not killed him... yet. Drachev looked up at the sounds of approaching tanks and American soldiers. Grabbing Alex's body, she tossed him out of the jeep and sped off into the desert moments before the soldiers arrived.

"He's just a kid..." one of the soldiers said in amazement as he beheld Alex Conroy.

"Wait, did he..." said another he was looked at the corpse of the monster.

"No... no it's impossible!" Edwards said as he surveyed the aftermath. Another convoy of military vehicles came to a stop in front of them, and a steaming mad, red mass known as General Jack Monroe flew out of a jeep and into Edward's face.

The last thing Alex remembered was hearing Monroe's voice and watching Drachev disappear into the darkness.

Alex wandered around his laboratory feeling well rested. The battle with the monster had taken its toll on him, and he had slept for days. His body was sore from the knocks and bruises that he had received, but he was happy. Alex smiled to see POPS walking around again, with gleaming, newly restored armor.

"Are you feeling better, Alex?"

"Much. And yourself, POPS?"

"All systems are running at one hundred percent efficiency."

"That's what I like to hear!"

Bounding down the stairs, Alex returned to his desk and looked at the notes he made before Monroe had called him into his office. He smiled and shook his head as he recalled his feeble attempts to move the table.

"After your battle with the monster, I doubt moving a desk will seem monumental."

"Yeah, well... what are they going to do with it?" Alex asked.

"They're taking the big bug over to Area 51 for study," Monroe answered as he entered the room, waving a lit cigar around. "I don't know what they're hoping to find, but at least it's out of our hair. Oh, and you'll be happy to know that that idiot Colonel got an earful from me."

"Well, he was only doing what he thought was best. I might have done the same thing." Alex shrugged forgivingly.

"Yeah, but disobeying direct orders do have their consequences. He'll be facing a disciplinary hearing very soon."

"Well, try to go easy on him."

"Based on General Monroe's psychological profile and previous conversations, there is a five percent chance that he will follow your advice." POPS chipped in.

"I see you're back to normal, metalhead." Monroe said as he rapped his knuckles against the robot's metal arm.

A thought occurred to Alex "And Agent Drachev, what about her?"

"Haven't found a trace of her since the final battle. We have the FBI looking, but with her skills as a spy... I'm not optimistic." Monroe shook his head.

"You're never optimistic!" Alex quipped.

"Yeah, you got that right." Monroe grunted as he inhaled his cigar. "If we ever do run across her again, well... I'd just like to know if she's for us or against us."

"I guess time will tell on that matter, sir." POPS spoke.

"Yeah, well... at least Adams... Schmidt... is behind bars. He's going to be facing trial for crimes against humanity. More than likely he'll cooperate. He'll give us all his research in exchange for some leniency. Leniency... he's even more deluded than I imagined! We're not Russia, we don't negotiate with evil!"

A grave expression appeared on Alex's face, he thought of what Drachev must be going through and then imagined more like her. "We ought to burn his research. His experiments must never hurt anyone again!"

"He's going to be put away for a long time Alex, no matter how he tries to butter us up!" Monroe said with a smile.

Alex breathed a sigh of relief as Monroe looked at the notes on the table.

"You can't move this little table, Ghost Boy?"

"Well..."

"Go on, Alex. I know you can." POPS said as he walked over to the table in question.

Feeling the pressure, Alex decided to make another attempt. After all, he was able to stop a tank bombardment; a simple metal table would pose no problem. He reached out with his mind...

...and the table stood still. Alex was stunned! He began to think of all the properties in the table, wondering if there was some element within or some hidden factor that he overlooked, but his thoughts were interrupted by POPS's monotone voice.

"Alex, perhaps your problem is that the table is bolted to the floor."

"Holy smokes! Are you kidding me!" Alex exclaimed as he leaped across his desk and dropped to the floor. Sure enough, POPS was right. Monroe walked over to Alex chuckling to himself.

"Well, boy genius you sure have outdone yourself this time." Monroe said slapping Alex across the back. He walked out of the laboratory with a great, big smile.

An embarrassed Alex turned to POPS with a grin on his face. "Well, Alex, at least you know that nothing is wrong with your powers." the robot said.

Alex got up, his mind on Pronux. To brave such a world where monsters like the insect existed, he must have been a courageous soul. Alex's powers, which he had questioned, were now a blessing to him. Pronux had died passing his abilities to the unborn Alex Conroy. Alex Conroy would not fail, Pronux's legacy will continue, brave and true. Inspired, Alex resolved to continue to use his extraordinary talents for the good of mankind, so that humanity will never create a monster such as the one from the nightmare world.

*THE END*

# IT CAME FROM
# THE 60s!

*I*first came across Ghost Boy when reading through Airship 27's hero bible. What could be more exciting than a spy teamed up with a robot? Yet when I started writing, I found this story to be quite a challenge. Ghost Boy is a departure from the average pulp hero since it takes place in the 60s. Obviously I was not around then, but one of my favorite things about that era were the Marvel comic books written by Stan Lee. He has always been one of my biggest heroes, and I wanted to capture the adventure and imagination from the Silver Age. I re-read many of my favorites to absorb the essence of what I wanted, and then I started to work.

I loved writing for the character POPS. Robots are among my favorite things ever, but there is something else I enjoy even more: monsters. So why not have POPS battle a monster from another world...having everything I love in one titanic story?

Of course, that led to the problem that I always struggle with: origins. Where did the monster come from? I felt that the monster had to resemble an American-style monster (I grew up loving the films of directors like Bert I. Gordon, Jack Arnold, and Nathan Juran) so I thought that an insect-like monster ravaging an Arizona town would be perfect. As for it's design, all I did was picture something that I would have liked to see Ray Harryhausen animate. That still left me with the problem of where it came from. Ron Fortier had sent me the origin comic for Ghost Boy, and I wanted to know more about Pronux's world. As a writer, I wondered what other creatures would live there. If there is anything that 1950's – 60's era science fiction movies taught us, it was that radiation causes creatures to grow to enormous size and attack cities. Therefore, I decided to make that the creature's origin: the radiation that destroyed Pronux's world created this beast.

Now I have to address a character that I loved writing for: Adela Drachev. James Bond movies of the 60's are a personal favorite, so I wanted to include a "Bond Girl" of my own in this story (hence the catsuit and gadget-enhanced sniper rifle). My first inclination was to make her a robot (she would be able to detect Ghost Boy through thermal vision, etc). However, I saw that another writer had created a Russian robot spy for Alex Conroy to contend with, and I did not wish to have Alex repeat this adventure (plus, somebody with his genius should be able to spot another cyborg). I liked the idea of Drachev being inhuman, but what other possibilities did I have? Racking my brain, I recalled viewing a tremendously powerful version of Frankenstein on stage with Benedict Cumberbatch and Johnny Lee Miller (I saw it streamed to theaters, not the actual stage mind you). In the play (as well as in the novel), Frankenstein created a beautiful female monster for the creature. I had always wondered what that character would have been like had she lived, and that's when it came to me. Drachev was a reanimated corpse!

To make her character more meaningful to the story, I wanted to give her a history with another character, and the only logical choice was General Jack Monroe. As a World War II veteran, I thought it would be interesting to expand on his backstory. I pictured Monroe would be the type of soldier to see everything through, and I thought of him cleaning up the concentration camps. Remembering the horrific experiments the Nazis inflicted on their prisoners, I thought that I had found a dark, yet fitting backstory for our mysterious spy. I could not see her working with the S.O.S., but I think it would be a delight to see her in other Ghost Boy adventures, thus I have her driving off into the night.

Alex Conroy was a little difficult for me to get the feel of at first, but I think the key to getting a story right is finding a problem that only *that* character could solve. I had to think of inventive ways for Ghost Boy to use his powers that may not have been used in other adventures. Once that was in place, re-reading Stan Lee's comics gave me the feel for the dialogue that I needed, plus I did my best to have him say "Holy smokes!" wherever I could.

I hope you have enjoyed this adventure, and I hope that I have made Bert I. Gordon, Jack Arnold, Nathan Juran, Stan Lee, and Ian Fleming proud.

∴ ∴

**ERIK FRANKLIN** - is a writer/actor/filmmaker based in Seattle. Recently graduating with honors from the Art Institute of Seattle in film production, he is the co-President of Franklin-Husser Entertainment LLC. He is working on two upcoming feature films for his company: A dinosaur action film "Revenge of the Lost" and the martial arts comedy "3 Morons Fighting Ninja". You can give the company page a "Like" at: https://www.facebook.com/pages/Franklin-Husser-Entertainment-LLC/290795021042906.

Drawn to pulp fiction through his love of history, literature, and Americana, he is grateful for Airship 27 Productions giving him the opportunity to write his first story. He looks forward to writing more adventures!

# THE SOUND OF OBEDIENCE
## BY LEE HOUSTON, JUNIOR

**P**rofessor Peter Patterson knew something was amiss the moment he awoke. "What's wrong?" he asked the three figures surrounding his bed.

"You will come with us," they said in unison, using an emotionless monotone voice, almost as if the three were artificial automatons and not living human beings.

"Why? Where?" he replied, while sitting up. Except for having removed his shoes, outer jacket, tie, and the contents of his pockets, Patterson was still dressed in the clothing he wore to church earlier that morning.

"For the glory of the Empire," said the tallest one, while brandishing a meat cleaver.

"For the glory of the Empire," repeated the other two, as they held up steak knives.

"You wouldn't," said Patterson in disbelief.

"Our orders are to take you alive, but lack of nonfatal injuries was never specified," said the group leader, moving the meat cleaver as if about to chop a finger off the Professor's hand.

"Okay. Okay. I'll cooperate," swore Patterson, as he started to climb out of bed. "Just don't hurt my family."

"Your desires are inconsequential. Only the Empire's matter," said the group leader.

"Only the Empire's," repeated the other two, as if but an echo of their commander.

With that, Patterson was led downstairs through his own home at knife point and escorted through the rear kitchen door to the backyard. There a van waited in the driveway, its engine idling.

Three men from inside the rear of the van got out its back doors. They were dressed alike in denim jeans and dark tee-shirts, as if employed in menial jobs. One moved menacingly toward Patterson, taking him from his initial kidnappers. The second carried a thick cord of rope and the third a rag that he began to pour something from a metal flask on.

Meanwhile, after conferring with the driver, another man came out the van's passenger side door. He was noticeably older than the others, with age lines around his mouth and eyes. The man's head was almost totally bald, except for some thin gray hair around the temples. He was attired much nicer than his companions in a suit and tie, which made Patterson assume he was the one in charge.

"What's going on here?" Patterson demanded to know. He could still see the driver sitting in the van, and was uncertain how many more people it might hold.

"Silence!" ordered the nicer dressed man, as the first two began binding Patterson's legs together, before they tied his hands behind his back. "While it is not my real name, you may call me Professor Toh, which is the closest translation to the word 'tone' from the proper Cyrillic alphabet to your inferior one," he said in a thick Russian accent. "My experiments here in your country are nearing completion, but I find myself in the rare position of needing a qualified assistant, which is why you're *volunteering*," he added with a sarcastic note in his voice.

"I will not cooperate!" said Patterson defiantly.

"You will, or else…" began Toh, while looking at the group that brought Patterson outside. With a simple nod of his head, each person raised their weapons to their throats. Then Toh turned back to face his captive and asked, "Shall I give them the order to finish the deed and commit suicide in front of you?"

"No," answered Patterson sadly. Then the third man's chloroform soaked rag was held over his mouth.

As Professor Patterson's unconscious form was loaded into the back of the van, Toh turned to his accomplices and said, "You did well. Now carry out the rest of your instructions."

"Yes sir," the three replied in unison, before going back inside the house.

With that, Toh climbed back into the passenger seat and the van left.

Ghost Boy, the public persona of an otherwise modest young scientist named Alex Conroy, had no solution for the problem before him. The assistant director of SOS operations stared at the disassembled, wall mounted control panel and wondered, *How did the kidnappers manage to bypass my security system?* At General Munroe's request, he had designed the system to protect those serving the United States who preferred to live off base so that their families could have some semblance of a normal life without a constant military presence nearby. With Alex's vast intellect and high security access to parts that were not commercially available to the average manufacturing company, the system was well above the current state of the art in home protection devices.

*The Pattersons didn't bother to leave it on after they came home from church, but that's understandable. No civilian would expect trouble under such peaceful conditions in broad daylight,* thought Ghost Boy, recalling the details of the hasty briefing given in route when the Science Operational Security division was called in to investigate the Professor's kidnapping. *It was the middle of the afternoon. Mrs. Patterson was in the kitchen fixing Sunday dinner and their children were in the living room listening to records on the family stereo after they set the table. Mister Patterson went upstairs for a nap. He never came down when called, and couldn't be found when searched for.*

Had it been turned on, the system would have registered the abductors as intruders and reported the situation back to the military base Alex Conroy called home immediately. Deactivated, the kidnappers would have at least registered as visitors, unwanted or otherwise.

However, the security system showed no one within the Patterson household at the time the Professor disappeared except the rest of the Patterson family.

*Mother, daughter, and son all swear they heard and saw nothing wrong while he was upstairs. Yet the system shows four people briefly going outside an hour before they discovered him missing, but only three coming back in. So if he was asleep the whole time…?*

"POPS," began Ghost Boy, turning to face the tall being next to him.

"I will perform another diagnostic scan if you request it," said Alex's mechanical friend and research assistant. "However, the results will be identical to all the previous examinations I have conducted. The security system is 100% completely functional. There is no evidence of outside tampering, power fluctuations, or other incongruities that might have affected its performance."

"Then I'm stymied," admitted the spectral scientist, as he began to put the control panel back together.

"Sorry to hear that," said General Munroe, their commanding officer and friend, as he came up behind his favorite operatives in the hallway between the living room and the kitchen.

"Any clue can be helpful," pointed out Ghost Boy. "I just don't know what this one might mean yet."

"That somebody on par with your capabilities is behind this?" wondered the General, in a low voice so the conversation remained between the three of them. "Could the kidnapper have flown Patterson out one of the upstairs windows?"

"Maybe," agreed Conroy, keeping his voice low too. "It was too nice a day to have them closed, but there's no evidence or system readings to support that theory. But if true, then why would whoever is behind this have needed a getaway vehicle and accomplices, or do you think those tire tracks and shoe prints our investigators found outside are just coincidence?" he asked, while replacing the plastic cover to complete the reassembly.

"The Pattersons own a sedan and a station wagon. Both of which are still in their garage. The sedan has a slight oil leak at the moment, and something drove through the stain it left in the driveway. The tire tracks don't match either car, so there was a third vehicle on the property at some point."

"Logical," agreed POPS, adjusting his artificial voice to match the others.

"The unaccounted for shoe prints in the dirt gutter alongside the driveway were of male work shoes, a left and a right. However they're two different sizes and both are too big to be either Patterson's or his son's. Besides, the evidence upstairs proves the Professor never was given time to put any shoes on before being taken," revealed the General.

"Meaning there was at least a driver and another kidnapper involved, as well as the fact that they wasted little time between accomplishing their goal and leaving," surmised Ghost Boy.

"How do you figure that?" asked Munroe.

"While there's nothing present to indicate the mastermind behind it all, there's definitely proof of advanced planning here. The villains obviously knew that Patterson and his family lived at the end of a quiet street in a residential neighborhood, so they waited until a Sunday afternoon to reduce their risk of discovery."

"Besides being taken shoeless, an indication of haste, there was always the possibility of someone being outside to do yard work, or neighbor children going out to play before dinner. The kidnappers probably disguised their vehicle in some manner to avoid suspicion if seen," added POPS.

"Makes sense," agreed the General. "Then we're looking for some kind of van, where it would be easy to keep whatever you don't want seen hidden in the back. So since it's Sunday, we're probably looking for some type of emergency household service, like a plumber, because something more major like an ambulance would have attracted too much attention, like our arrival has. Anything else?"

"I didn't get a chance to do it earlier, because I wanted to check out the alarm system, but I'd like to interview the family too," said Ghost Boy.

"Sure," said Munroe. "Are you going to..." and then his voice trailed off, while the General tapped the side of his head, indicating his friend's telepathic abilities.

"Discretely," acknowledged Conroy. "By the way, what does Professor Patterson do?"

"He's our foremost sound engineer. Right now, he's been working on improving all our communications gear. We need the best equipment possible if we're going to keep President Kennedy's promise of reaching the moon by the end of this decade."

"Understood," said Ghost Boy tersely. The fact that he was away on another mission and nowhere near Dallas, Texas that fateful day still bothered him. Whether or not he would have been successful in saving a good man's life was a question whose elusive answer might always haunt him.

"Okay. Let's go," Alex said to POPS, as he stored his portable tool pouch within an outer pocket of the white lab coat he wore.

As America's amazing agent entered the living room, he quickly took in the scene before him. The three of them sat together on the sofa that occupied most of one wall. Ghost Boy's telepathy revealed that all were worried about the safety and whereabouts of the Professor, but that each member of the Patterson family also had individual concerns at the moment.

*Did I remember to turn the oven off? I don't want the roast to dry out,* wondered Mrs. Patterson, as she nervously chewed on an unpolished fingernail and stared at her children, worried what would become of them if the worst happened. Other than having switched to more comfortable shoes, with the string of pearls she only wore on family outings no longer around her neck since donning an apron, she was still wearing her Sunday go-to-meeting dress.

Her young son Jeffery sat next to his mother, wearing the clean jeans and t-shirt that he changed into after returning home. Barely into his thirteenth year, the boy leaned forward as far as he could and still be considered sitting on the couch, to stare at POPS. *Cool robot! What makes it tick?* he asked himself, unhappy that he couldn't go grab some tools from his father's garage workbench and find out.

*Ghost Boy is so dreamy,* older daughter Jennifer thought to herself, which made Alex momentarily blush. She wore a dress almost like her mother's, except that hers accented the fact she had the curves of a beautiful young woman. Miss Patterson was a freshman at the local university, although uncertain what she wanted to major in.

The boy sported an unruly brown mop of hair like his father, with a slight touch of freckles under his eyes. The ladies were both blondes, and Alex could see where Jennifer got her good looks from, but concentrated on the matter at hand.

After reintroducing himself and POPS, Ghost Boy started the conversation by reassuring the family. "We're doing everything we can to get Mister Patterson back home as quickly as possible, but maybe you folks can assist with that. Is there anything you might have thought of since you first talked with General Munroe that could possibly help us?"

"Like what?" asked Jennifer, staring at him intently.

"Maybe you saw or heard something that you didn't think much of at the time, but are questioning now?"

His suggestive inquiry caused the Pattersons to stop and individually go back over the events of the day. Ghost Boy carefully scanned their thoughts, hoping there might be some new information that either wasn't remembered or thought unimportant before. However, while each person's memories remained true to their previous statements, there was something amongst them that wasn't quite right.

*For some reason, all three of them can mentally picture Professor Patterson walking outside and disappearing into thin air, as if they might have actually witnessed the kidnapping. Yet they also react like they were powerless to stop it and don't want to remember any specific details. How is that possible?*

Conroy continued his interview by questioning each family member individually, starting with the wife, when Jeffery suddenly announced, "I'm bored. Do you mind if I turn on the stereo and listen to some more records?"

Both women started to admonish him, but Ghost Boy said it would be okay. He wanted the family loose and relaxed in hopes that they might recall something.

Having a grownup's permission, Jeffery went to the built-in wall shelves across from the couch and started going through the family's record collection, when he saw something odd.

*What's Jen's new album doing by the waste basket?* he asked himself, while bending down to retrieve it. *Must not have made it back on the shelf with all the others she had out earlier,* was Jeffery's best guess, as he took the vinyl disc out of its protective cover and placed the record on the turntable.

As the first track on Side One started to play in high fidelity stereo sound, the youngest Patterson rejoined the rest of his family on the couch.

Mrs. Patterson tried to be helpful, and Ghost Boy knew she had answered every question truthfully, but there was no further, let alone useful information. She was starting to develop a sense of detachment that Alex concluded was the onset of fatigue, caused by today's stressful events. When the second song finished, Mrs. Patterson asked if she could be excused for a moment.

Seeing no reason not to honor the request, Conroy agreed. He watched long enough to see her heading through the dining room into the kitchen, then turned his attention back to questioning the children. "So, can you recall anything unusual that might of happened today?"

Jeffery just shook his head negatively.

"There was... one... thing..." replied Jennifer, as her voice trailed off.

"What?" Ghost Boy asked eagerly, not noticing the far away stare now on Jeffery's face.

"Children," said Mrs. Patterson in an authoritative tone as she reentered the living room.

"Yes mother," the daughter and son said in unison, suddenly sitting up straight.

"It is time to capture Professor Patterson for the glory of the Empire. After we deal with those who would try to stop us," announced Mrs. Patterson in a monotone voice, as she held up a meat cleaver in her right hand and two steak knives in her left, obtained from the kitchen.

"For the glory of the Empire," repeated the children, as they stood up in unison like soldiers. Ghost Boy couldn't help noting that their voices now sounded more emotionless than POPS' artificially produced speech.

"POPS," began Conroy, as he placed himself between the children and their mother.

"Analysis scan initiated," announced the metallic companion, while placing himself in a defensive position between Alex and Mrs. Patterson. "I am detecting an unusual, low level frequency transmission, originating from the record player."

"Inform General Munroe and request his return," Ghost Boy ordered POPS, while reaching down to pick up a decorative coaster with a thin marble base from the coffee table. As he briefly turned to face the stereo system, the fourth song was coming to an end. Alex quickly figured out the logistics in his head and flung the coaster like a mini Olympic discus toward the record player.

The makeshift missile hit its target accurately and forced the tone arm to the end of the album, creating a scratching noise for all to hear over the stereo speakers as the phonograph needle rapidly crossed the final two tracks. The coaster remained on the record, continuously circling around on the turntable with the album as the tone arm rose above the vinyl disc. The bracket swung back to rest in its cradle on the right hand side of the player, then the turntable automatically shut itself off.

However, the three enthralled people still tried to carry out their mission.

"Out of my way!" Mrs. Patterson ordered POPS. "You cannot stop the glory of the Empire," she declared in a louder, but still flat voice. In her dazed state, she never realized the true nature of her opponent and swung the meat cleaver at POPS' head, while she thrust the steak knives toward his chest.

At a height of seven feet, Ghost Boy's artificial ally was much taller than the housewife. The stainless steel knife tips broke against his far more durable body as POPS grabbed one of his assailant's wrists within each of his strong hands to restrain her. Enough pressure was applied to make Mrs. Patterson drop the meat cleaver and what remained of the steak knives, but was insufficient to hurt delicate human flesh.

Meanwhile, Ghost Boy wasn't faring as well against the Patterson children. He had to grab both of Jennifer's hands to keep her from attempting to claw his face like a rabid wildcat with her manicured fingernails. This act left him defenseless as Jeffery caught him by surprise. The son kicked Ghost Boy in the left shin as hard as he could.

Instinct made the spectral scientist lift his left leg, as the possessed Patterson boy attempted repeating his attack against the right leg. Alex pushed Jennifer away with both hands before reaching out to grab her brother. Ghost Boy shoved the boy harder than he did the daughter. Caught by surprise, Jeffery stumbled backward and landed on the couch.

Jennifer, while pushed back a step or two, had not lost her balance. She used the distraction caused by her brother and attempted to kick Ghost Boy in a more personal place. However, Alex Conroy momentarily turned intangible, proving the accuracy of his public code name.

As he contemplated his next move, Alex's shin started to ache, and knew it would require an ice pack and some time in an elevated position to heal properly. Yet he also knew that the Pattersons were not responsible for their current actions. *How can we stop them without either hurting an innocent victim or being injured ourselves?*

Momentum made Jennifer Patterson stumble forward, right through her opponent. As she recovered her balance, the daughter couldn't comprehend what happened in her current mental state. Not seeing her enemy, she looked ahead and saw the person she now thought of as her team leader being held captive by POPS, totally unaware that Ghost Boy was right behind her.

Conroy turned and grabbed the daughter by her slim waist with both arms before she could launch a surprise attack against his computerized companion that would hurt her more than POPS. Caught off guard, Jennifer made no effort to fight back as he picked her up and spun around so that they faced the couch again.

"I don't understand," said Ghost Boy, quickly filling his partner in on what his telepathy revealed, as he struggled to keep Jennifer from either stomping one of her shoe heels into his feet or kicking him without turning intangible again. "The memories were probably deeply repressed, which is why my initial telepathic scans revealed what they did, but why are the Pattersons still trying to reenact the Professor's kidnapping? I stopped the record."

"Having already heard it once, they are probably working from those repressed memories to carry out the instructions, not realizing they have already been successful," replied Conroy's comrade, while bodily lifting Mrs. Patterson into the air to keep her from duplicating Jeffery's shin kicking trick. If she had made contact with POPS' metallic limbs, she would only have succeeded in shattering every bone in her foot.

"What this family lacks in actual training, they make up for in a single minded determination to carry out—OW!" screamed Alex, as Jennifer managed to turn her head enough to bite him in the upper arm as hard as she could. Although painful, a later examination would reveal she never broke the skin. Conroy managed to hang on to the possessed woman, who was still struggling to break free. "There's only one thing I can do," realized Ghost Boy, as he used his telepathic power again.

The next instant, the Patterson family went limp, obeying the mentally planted suggestion to take a nap. The women fell into unconsciousness within their opponent's arms while Jeffery Patterson, who was about to jump off the sofa in another attempt to attack Alex, fell back onto the cushions.

"Help me get them back into their sitting positions before Jeffery wanted to play the stereo," requested Ghost Boy, as he dragged Jennifer to the couch.

"I got POPS' radio message. What's your status?" asked General Munroe, as he reentered the living room from the dining room, via the back door, with two more soldiers at his side. Their sidearms were drawn, but holstered after quickly eying the situation. All seemed secure. The Pattersons were asleep on the sofa, with POPS standing guard over them.

Ghost Boy straightened his lab coat and ran a hand through his ruffled blonde locks before speaking. "We have some of the kidnappers in custody," he reported, before explaining in greater detail.

"How's that possible?" the General demanded to know, after dismissing the other men.

"This is the culprit," revealed Conroy, as he walked over to the stereo and took the record off the turntable to present Munroe. Then he started looking for its cardboard cover and interior paper sleeve.

The General stared at the vinyl disc. It looked like any normal thirty-three and a third long playing record to him. While Munroe didn't doubt Ghost Boy's report, sometimes he needed further, more detailed explanations to completely comprehend some of the fantastic things they experienced. "Are you sure there isn't some gizmo hidden in the record player itself?"

"I already double checked that theory, but there's no evidence to support it. Given the pretty spotless conditions around here, Mrs. Patterson obviously cleans house on a regular basis, but she's never thought to move

" HELP ME GET THEM BACK INTO THEIR SITTING POSITIONS
BEFORE JEFFREY WANTED TO PLAY THE STEREO, "

the stereo components and dust either underneath or behind them," said Alex, briefly picking up the turntable to show the accumulated dust in that area hadn't been disturbed in ages. "Therefore, no one has messed with their stereo system beyond normal use."

"Well, none of the Pattersons seem like the type to go looking for them, but I've heard some scuttlebutt about how some recording artists are allegedly hiding messages in their music that can only be found if the record is played backwards. Yet I've never believed any of that hooey before now, let alone heard of it being capable of making someone do anything like this," added Munroe, while staring at the sleeping victims.

"I don't know whether or not that reverse recording practice is true General, but this is different," replied Ghost Boy. "What we're dealing with here is a serious form of subliminal messaging."

"Which is?" the superior officer asked in return, because he didn't know the term.

"It happens on a more subtle level, like being unaware of a very low whisper, even if the person speaking is standing right next to you," explained POPS. "You are discretely being told to believe or do something, but are unaware of ever hearing the message even when you do act upon it." Then the amazing automaton excused himself and left the room.

"Sometimes an advertising agency is suspected of using subliminal messaging to secretly manipulate people to favor certain products over others," added Conroy, "but the basic concept is being taken to the extreme in this instance."

"What? You mean brain washing?" asked Munroe.

"Exactly, and obviously very powerful too, considering the Pattersons probably only heard this doctored album for the first time today. Otherwise, the Professor would have been taken much earlier."

"Just because of a record?" repeated the General, staring at the disc as if how the task was accomplished could be seen with the naked eye.

"I'll have to take the album back to the laboratory for further analysis, but the obvious clue is here on the record label. See?" asked Ghost Boy, pointing to the upper half of the round decal in the center of the vinyl disc.

"*The Insects: Assistance*," read Munroe aloud. "So? They're a popular group. I hear their music being played around the base during some of the younger soldiers off duty hours. Within regulations, of course."

"Yes, but now examine the album cover," requested his friend, holding it up next to the record.

The General looked and saw a color photograph of four relatively clean cut young men, all dressed in black suits, standing in a green field waving their arms about like they were birds or bugs. "I don't get it. What's wrong?" he asked.

"The group spells their name as you see on the cover: I-N-S-E-K-T-S. Now look at the label again."

"The name's spelled properly with a C."

"Exactly. Whoever is behind this either stole or bought a legitimate album, and then made a copy that they put their subliminal messaging into, but never noticed the uniqueness of the band's name," explained Conroy, as he put the record back in its sleeve.

"We'll start checking every possible recording studio in the area where this fake album might have been made first thing in the morning," said the General, anxious to find Professor Patterson.

Ghost Boy was about to say something when Mrs. Patterson began to moan.

"They're starting to come around," observed Alex, as her daughter began to physically shutter, as if having a bad nightmare.

"Will they remember any of this? Let alone anything that might help us find the Professor?" asked Munroe.

"I hated doing it, but when I rendered them unconscious, I left the command in their minds that they would recall everything upon awakening," revealed Conroy. "Whether or not that includes anything useful remains to be seen."

As Jeffery Patterson began to stir, POPS returned to the living room carrying a serving tray. On it were a pitcher of ice water and three glasses obtained from the kitchen, along with a bottle of aspirin found in the first floor guest bathroom's medicine cabinet. "I calculated high odds that the Pattersons might suffer some physical after effects from a second possession, especially in light of their forced release," he said, as Mrs. Patterson suddenly sat upright with a start.

"What have we done?" she asked in a state of shock, before she began to cry.

"It wasn't your fault ma'am," said the General reassuringly, as he searched the living room in hopes of finding a box of tissues. Meanwhile, POPS handed her a glass of freshly poured ice water and two aspirin.

"But those men, especially that Professor Tone with that thick Russian accent of his," added the housewife, while trying to wipe the tears from her eyes.

"Tone?" asked Munroe, looking at Conroy and POPS.

"She probably means Toh," said Ghost Boy, pronouncing the surname correctly, before giving the General a brief explanation of the Cyrillic alphabet.

"I remember him complaining about our alphabet and saying that wasn't his real name," added Mrs. Patterson, after accepting a handkerchief from the General, since Munroe couldn't locate any tissues.

POPS searched through the SOS files that he was authorized to carry in his memory banks, but found no known enemy operative using that alias.

"What will they do to my husband?" Mrs. Patterson demanded to know, as her children fully regained consciousness.

He awoke to find himself surrounded by a darkness that was broken only by the dim light of a single bulb from somewhere overhead. Discovering that he was tied to a chair, the man instinctively sought a way to escape as he heard a voice say, "First off Professor Patterson, I must apologize. My... associate was inexperienced and used too much chloroform. He has been... disciplined for the mistake, and I sincerely hope you are suffering no ill effects from the experience."

"Let me go," Patterson demanded, struggling against his bonds.

"That is no way for a learned man like yourself to behave," said Professor Tone, as he came into view. He waited until someone still in the darkness placed a chair behind him, and then sat down in front of his prisoner. "When our experiments are over, you shall be free to leave and do whatever you wish." *That I command,* he added silently.

"I'll never help the enemy," Patterson said defiantly.

"A commendable attitude, within reason," admitted Tone. "If our positions were reversed, I would probably feel the same. But surely you have realized by now that you have no options available, except to cooperate."

"What do you want?" the captive asked.

"You have seen my new method of... persuasion in action," said Tone, sitting back in his chair as if having a casual conversation with a colleague. "The process works, but alas it still has limitations. You will cooperate fully to help me overcome those hindrances, or else," he added menacingly.

"Or else, what?" Patterson demanded to know.

"Need I remind you that, despite the fact we are nowhere within their immediate vicinity, the fate of your wife and children still rests within my hands?" asked Tone, leaning slightly forward in his chair to let the Professor fully see the evil expression on his face. "Instead of ordering them all to commit suicide, after a few specially crafted and well placed messages, I could make your son Jeffery a juvenile delinquent. As for your wife and daughter..."

Tone let his voice trail off, allowing Patterson to shudder as he imagined the worst possible scenario.

Jennifer started complaining of a "wicked headache", while Jeffery simply cradled his head in both hands and moaned.

Each sibling accepted POPS' generous offer of relief as they poured themselves a drink and took a dose of aspirin.

Using the opportunity to avoid answering Mrs. Patterson's last question, the SOS personnel waited until after the Pattersons looked and felt a little better before resuming the interview.

"Please tell us what you can remember," requested Ghost Boy in a gentle voice.

Mrs. Patterson began recounting everything, with the children adding additional details where they could.

"I started hearing this voice, as if I was listening to a ghost. No offense," she told Ghost Boy.

"None taken," said Alex.

"Anyway, I couldn't figure out where the voice was coming from, let alone who was speaking," said the housewife, as her children nodded in agreement. "I was to arm the children and myself to force what the voice claimed was this evil man out of our good home. Then I was to call a specific phone number and report that we were ready to proceed."

"What was the number?" asked the General.

Mrs. Patterson answered, "555-"

"-0264 is assigned to a pay telephone three blocks from here," announced POPS moments later, after another quick internal memory search. "It is located on the corner of a full service filling station that is closed Sundays."

"They probably sat there in the van, waiting for the phone to ring, which would then confirm that the Pattersons had listened to the record and were obeying orders," said Ghost Boy.

"I'll have the phone dusted for fingerprints and canvas the area in case anyone saw anything," added General Munroe. *It's a long shot, but we might get lucky.*

"We were to capture 'the enemy', and then take him to the backyard, where government security men would be waiting in a van to take him away," revealed Jeffery. "At the time, I was told it was cool to do this. That I was helping my country get rid of a wanted criminal."

"But we were really helping the Reds kidnap Dad!" realized Jennifer. "The one phrase that kept getting repeated over and over was 'For the glory of the Empire'. Why didn't we know what was really going on?"

"Because none of this is your fault. You were being brainwashed by subliminal messages on this," explained Ghost Boy, before showing them the falsified album. "Where did you get it?"

"From this older looking guy in a suit," said Jennifer.

"How old?" asked General Munroe.

"Much older looking than my dad, because he didn't have all his hair, and most of what was there had turned gray," she replied. "He was parked near the church after Sunday services today in a different van than the one that took Dad, handing out records. There were multiple copies of several currently popular albums being given away. The man was just handing them out, with no apparent strings attached. Said it was a promotion for a new radio station that would be coming on the air soon. You can imagine the clamor to get one."

"The current price of a record album, multiplied by…" began POPS.

"It was a rhetorical question," Ghost Boy said to his friend.

"Anyway, the man seemed nice enough, but insisted on giving me that specific record," recalled Jennifer. "I remember that now, because it had a yellow dot on the plastic wrapping that none of the others he was passing out did. You'll find that in the waste basket near the stereo."

As POPS went to retrieve the evidence for further study, Jeffery asked, "Say, why was that record by the trash can anyway?"

"Because I was ordered to get rid of it after we came back inside from kidnapping Dad, and then forget everything we did, but part of me found that hard to do," answered his sister.

"Why?" wondered Ghost Boy.

"Don't you know how popular *The Insekts* are right now, let alone how hard it is to get their albums?" Jennifer asked in return.

"No, I don't," admitted Alex.

"What?" said Jennifer, honestly surprised. "Are you living in a cave or something?"

"It's actually a military base laboratory," was Ghost Boy's response.

"Well, we have to get you away from those stuffy old test tubes and out in the real world more often," replied Jennifer with genuine interest, as she stared at Alex intently with her deep blue eyes.

"Can you describe the van?" asked Munroe, trying to get the conversation back onto more important topics.

Jennifer turned to look at the General and said, "They were both white. Only four doors. Two normal ones up front with large side mirrors and two cargo doors in the rear. No side doors and only the front end had clear glass. The back windows were painted over. The one that took Dad had no signage at all. The one after church displayed advertising for radio station K-FUN all over it."

Conroy and Munroe both turned to look at POPS, who started the necessary search without even being asked. "My internal memory banks show that there are radio stations licensed to use the call letters K-F-U-N in both New Mexico and California, but none in Arizona," answered the mechanical marvel moments later. "The Federal Communications Commission has received no applications for either establishing a new radio station, or changing the call sign of an existing station within the state of Arizona for well over a calendar year."

"Well, that's a dead end," said Ghost Boy, with a hint of disappointment in his voice.

"Maybe not. Obviously the villains ripped all the advertising off that vehicle between the two events instead of taking the risk of stealing another one," realized the General. "I can have local authorities see if either station is missing a van. Then we'd at least know where the enemy came from, and that might give us a clue as to how they intend to leave the country again when whatever they're planning is done."

"Okay. Now I would like everyone to relax and clear their heads," Ghost Boy requested of the Pattersons. "As soon as we can find some paper and pencils, I would like you to start describing to me everything you can remember about the men you met in the backyard."

Over an hour later Conroy completed the last sketch, using his telepathic abilities to help him fill in details that the Pattersons couldn't accurately describe, but clearly saw in their memories. While no one got a good look at the van's driver, the henchmen were rather generic looking criminal assistants. *Perhaps even local hoodlums. The damn traitors,* thought General Munroe.

After he showed it to the Pattersons, each family member agreed Ghost Boy's drawing of the man known only as Professor Toh was 100% accurate. However, the SOS staff had a different response.

"Obviously Russian, but I don't remember seeing this guy in any dossier, regardless of what alias he's using," said General Munroe, after taking another, good hard look at the picture when they had a chance to converse alone. The family was now in the kitchen. Despite their protests of not being hungry, Mrs. Patterson insisted on making sure her children had something for dinner, although her original pot roast plans were now canceled.

"His image matches no scan within my memory banks," added POPS.

"Great. Another new player," commented Ghost Boy with a bit of disgust in his voice.

"I know the feeling Alex," whispered Munroe. "They're like bad pennies. Take care of one and another turns up."

"I just wish I could spend more time in the lab than out in the field fighting bad guys," admitted Conroy, thinking about all the experiments and lines of scientific investigation he had yet to pursue. "Well, we've done all we can here," conceded Ghost Boy. "Better head back to the base so I can start examining what evidence we do have," he added, while picking up the record off the coffee table.

After a hearty breakfast in the Officer's Mess the next morning, General Munroe grabbed the file lying next to his tray and, after personally policing his area instead of letting the enlisted man on duty do it, went to Ghost Boy's private laboratory. Passing the exterior security checkpoint, he went inside to find, as usual, that Alex Conroy was so absorbed in his work, last night's dinner sat on a side table, barely touched.

"It's reassuring to see that while the more things change, the more they stay the same," commented Munroe, as POPS tried to convince Alex to pause long enough to eat some of the breakfast that the General had sent over.

"You know how he is," was POPS' only reply, as he set the mess hall tray down next to the uneaten dinner. "At least he conceded to elevating and icing his left leg while he worked, so it is better now."

"We should probably install a refrigerator in here to keep some food on hand," observed Munroe.

"Alex will only use it to preserve more specimens, just like he did with the last two," presumed POPS.

Ignoring their comments, the subject of their conversation announced his findings.

"Whoever this Professor Toh, or Tone is; the man is on to something," conceded Conroy, as he looked up at the General. "Current brainwashing techniques require prolonged physical contact with the target, if not chemicals as well. The biggest advantages his technique has are subtlety and the element of surprise to subjugate a person's will while unaware that they are being brainwashed. In this case, if the subliminal messages weren't directed at the Pattersons specifically, they would have affected anyone in that living room who heard them."

"Oh? How?" asked Munroe, now even more concerned about what the enemy might do next.

"Tone simply addressed them individually when issuing his instructions. Probably to make sure he had their attention. He made a copy of the original album, while including an additional audio track on both sides, in case someone decided to play Side B first instead of A. That side's now a tad garbled toward the end because of my abrupt stopping of the record player, but here's a transcript of what the Pattersons were told to do from B," said Alex, while handing Munroe a typewritten report. "There were even instructions for Professor Patterson himself, in case he was in the living room when the record was played."

"Hmmm..." said the General, as he looked over the pages. "The Professor would have called that number himself and surrendered voluntarily if he heard it."

"What saved him was being upstairs asleep at the time. Obviously Patterson's been kidnapped to help Tone perfect the technique's effectiveness, if not its range of influence as well," added Alex.

"Then it can be overcome?" asked Munroe, hopeful of a favorable answer.

"That depends upon when you make the attempt," admitted Conroy. "We have identified and isolated the low level audio frequency that the subliminal messages were recorded and hidden in the album on. That is both his technique's strength, as demonstrated by its effectiveness, and its Achilles' Heel. Because Tone is using such a low frequency, it can't travel over a great distance without the risk of being distorted and garbling the message. Otherwise, any standard pair of ear plugs or ear muffs will protect the listener from succumbing, unless they've already heard the instructions."

"Then once they've been exposed to the message, they obey without question?" the General asked, dreading the answer.

"Depending upon how much of the orders have already been heard," answered POPS. "If for some reason the transmission is incomplete, our theory is that the subject will either only carry out what they can, or wait until they hear the complete broadcast before complying."

"Or the enemy could intentionally delay the remainder of the instructions until the right opportunity presented itself," added Conroy.

"Which would make anyone the perfect covert agent," realized Munroe. "Not even the patsy would be aware of what was going on. Think of the implications!"

Alex agreed. "Overall, a well thought out scheme, and if there's room for improvement—"

"But we have discovered a few flies in the ointment," revealed the General, while setting the report back down on the work bench.

"Oh?" asked Conroy, turning to look at his friend with greater interest.

"The local authorities have identified one of the kidnappers. His body was found in an industrial trash dumpster behind that filling station this morning by a grease monkey a little after oh-six hundred, while they were preparing to open for the day."

Ghost Boy shook his head in disbelief. "The man must have done something to really anger Tone, who is probably a very strict disciplinarian too."

From the file he brought with him, Munroe laid out a copy of a photograph from the local police department, along with a copy of Conroy's drawing of one of the kidnapping suspects. They were identical, except for the clothing. The law enforcement image showed the suspect wearing a striped prison uniform, while Ghost Boy just drew a few simple lines to represent a t-shirt.

"Joesph Gould was strangled by an as yet unidentified assailant before being discarded like yesterday's trash," said the General, reciting details from the police report that was delivered while he had breakfast. "A local, but career criminal. In and out of the Arizona state penitentiary system numerous times. All minor felonies, with no sentence lasting more than a year at most, until now."

"Known associates?" asked Alex, while looking at the photo.

"Michael Staton and Chester Curtis," answered the General, while pulling out copies of their police photographs along with Ghost Boy's sketches, before setting the images down on the table in pairs. Like Gould's, the two pictures of each man were perfect matches other than their attire. "That gives us everybody but the driver and Professor Tone himself," he added. "The police have All Points Bulletins out for them now, but at our request, will only report their location if spotted."

"Giving us a chance to rescue Professor Patterson and apprehend Tone," assumed Conroy.

"Yes," confirmed Munroe. "My theory is that Tone came into the country alone, maybe even on a legitimate passport somehow. Then once he got here, recruited locally."

"Traveling alone would make him less conspicuous," confirmed POPS. "Thankfully, the hoodlums are not enemy agents themselves. They might not even know Professor Toh's a Russian spy."

"They're still guilty of aiding and abetting," said the General.

"I wonder if they know their friend's dead?" asked Alex. "Might make a difference in what they do next."

"Don't know. Meanwhile, the California radio station is the one missing a van, meaning our head Red on this operation came in from the west coast," said Munroe, as he saw the faraway expression appear on Conroy's face. Alex was lost in thought.

"I know that look," said the General. "What is it?"

"We already know that, as part of his scheme, Tone needed to make a copy of the real record to doctor it with his subliminal messages. What if he has access to a radio station here?" asked Alex.

"Would they even have the necessary equipment to do that?" asked Munroe in return.

"We're not talking mass production here. Just the need to make an occasional album, or in this case, copy," replied Conroy. "They certainly have recording equipment for commercials, promotional spots, and stuff like that. Yet, because the invention of the magnetic tape format in Germany wasn't discovered until *after* World War Two, such events were either done live or pre-recorded. The materials to make an album have changed over the years, yet..."

"We can still search local radio stations that were active when I was your age," realized Munroe.

"I have already compiled a list," announced POPS, moving to write down the information.

"Good. I already have teams deployed checking out recording studios.

"KNOWN ASSOCIATES?" ASKED ALEX, WHILE LOOKING AT THE PHOTO.

We can start investigating the radio stations after the briefing," said General Munroe, as he started gathering up his photographs.

"What briefing?" asked Alex.

General Munroe, along with an armed escort, walked with Ghost Boy and POPS toward the central command building to meet with base personnel at oh-nine hundred. The topic of conversation was to be bringing everyone up to date on the search and rescue efforts concerning Professor Peter Patterson.

Unfortunately, the enemy had other plans.

As they traveled along the gravel road past the mess hall's kitchen, General Munroe recognized the sweet sounds of one of his favorite singers crooning a tune. *Now that's good music, so I won't chastise the cook too harshly for having the radio on so loud,* he thought to himself.

Alex Conroy stopped in mid-step. The soldier positioned in the rear of the group almost walked into him. Ghost Boy responded by turning around and slugging the man in face as hard and fast as possible.

Stunned, the soldier fell to the ground as Alex moved to continue his unprovoked attack against the remaining escorts.

"Ghost Boy, what..." began General Munroe, only to have POPS supply the answer.

"He has fallen under Professor Tone's control," came the announcement Munroe dreaded hearing. "The message is coming over that radio broadcast."

As the other sentries attempted to restrain their possessed ally, Munroe grabbed the soldier closest to him and started issuing orders.

"Put the base on full alert immediately! Nobody in or out without my authorization! Every possible effort is to be made to stop Ghost Boy without using weaponry. He's only possessed by an outside force and can't help himself right now. And turn off all outside communications. Especially radios!" demanded the General. "Raid both the firing range and the winter stores for supplies, but I want all personnel issued ear plugs *and* ear muffs! Hopefully Ghost Boy was the only target of this attack, although that's bad enough. Then tell our communications division to start homing in on..."

POPS shouted out the exact low level audio frequency used by Professor Tone, even as he grabbed Alex's wrists.

"Any broadcast at that frequency. I want a mobile tracking unit, with jamming equipment, and a fully armed combat team ready to deploy as soon as I join them. Understood?" asked Munroe, as the last member of their escort fell unconscious in a losing battle against Ghost Boy.

"Yes, sir!" shouted the soldier, pausing only long enough to salute, before running off to comply with the General's orders.

With only POPS and himself left to face off against a mind controlled Alex Conroy, Munroe didn't hesitate to pull out his military issued sidearm. It was only after the gun cleared his holster that the General swung it around in his hand so that the butt was facing outward, before he approached his friends, squaring off against each other.

"Back away!" Ghost Boy shouted at POPS, yet his voice sounded quite emotionless. It was akin to the way the Pattersons spoke when possessed, like a helpless drone. "For the honor of the Empire, I must destroy this base before joining my superiors and aid their glorious plans for world domination."

"You do not want to do that Alex," said POPS calmly. Besides possessing a psychological advantage, it was currently safe to use Ghost Boy's real name, since the two of them and General Munroe were the only ones in the immediate area still conscious. "You are a good man, who is only being ordered to do something he should not."

"Who's this Alex character?" Conroy demanded to know. "I'm Ghost Boy, scourge of the free world!" he added, almost proud of the lie.

"No, you are not," stated POPS. "Now think about…"

"Let me go!" yelled Ghost Boy, as he started frantically trying to pull out of POPS' grasp.

General Munroe let POPS take point while he tried to sneak up behind Ghost Boy.

*Thankfully he doesn't know his true identity, but that Tone character has really done a number on Alex,* realized Munroe, as he covertly came up behind his friend. *When I get my hands on him,* the General promised himself, as he raised his gun.

The plan was to knock Conroy unconscious, using the weapon like a blackjack. Then, after securing Ghost Boy, hope that POPS could find a way to break the evil Professor's grip on Alex before tracking down the villain and kicking his butt red, white, and blue.

Unfortunately, as much as Munroe admired his friend's abilities, he was rarely ever on the opposing side of them.

Realizing the delicate nature of human flesh, POPS was forced to release Alex before he suffered more than mild bruising around the wrists.

Alex turned and hit the General as hard as he could with his right fist, while the left hand reached out and grabbed Munroe's gun before the man could react.

"You forgot I can read minds, didn't you?" gloated Ghost Boy, as he transferred the weapon to his right hand and switched the safety off. "Threatening Professor Toh, my superior officer, is a severe offense, punishable by death. You don't like being on the receiving end of military justice, do you General Munroe?" he asked, while holding the weapon properly, with the barrel pointed at Munroe's head.

A normal Alex Conroy would never find himself within such a situation, aiming a gun at not only an innocent man, but at a close friend of his as well. A mind controlled Ghost Boy never hesitated as he started to squeeze the trigger, relishing the thought of being able to rid the Empire of a hated enemy.

However, the bullet was never discharged, for an artificial hand surrounded the barrel and crushed it.

As he dropped the now worthless handgun, a confused Alex turned to confront POPS once more as General Munroe grabbed him from behind.

As he watched the General try to confront Ghost Boy, POPS saw it necessary to render the base commander some assistance.

There was no satisfaction in hearing the crunch of the gun barrel, only an acknowledgment of accomplishment as the robotic associate calculated the best course of action in response to the current situation as the General grabbed Alex from behind.

The older man's arms slipped around Conroy's chest, before coming up over his shoulders. Munroe's fingers interlocked behind Ghost Boy's head while Conroy braced his feet and attempted to break away from his attacker.

"I can tell your heart isn't in this battle General Munroe," said Alex, with what appeared to be genuine feeling. "We've known each other for years. You've seen me grow up and think of me at least as a friend, if not something more familial. But guess what? My heart is *completely* in this battle!" added Conroy, as he put his whole weight and effort into bending forward, lifting Munroe up off the ground in the process.

The General suddenly found himself flying over Ghost Boy, who dropped down on one knee to allow him clear passage. Munroe landed on his keister at POPS' feet, with thankfully the only injury being to his pride.

"This is too easy," bragged Conroy, watching his newfound enemies just stay where they were and stare at him. "When I was your dupe Munroe, you always depended upon me to save you and this worthless country. But do you want to know the truth? You fools relied on me for so long it's made you weaker than you were before me! Meanwhile, I was just lying in wait until the day I could carry out my *real* mission for my *true* superiors.

"And you..." continued Ghost Boy, looking at POPS.

The mechanical man silently prepared himself. While whatever Ghost Boy was about to say might hurt an organic being with human emotions, POPS was fully aware that in the end any statement would only be hollow words with no true logical meaning, despite whatever possessed Conroy to say them.

Yet for whatever reason, Alex never finished his sentence. He paused, shaking his head as if trying to clear it, then picked up where he left off. "The only way I'm going to prove my value to the Empire is to end this assignment quicker than they thought it would take," said Ghost Boy, as he started to run in the opposite direction, away from his confused friends.

"Alex did not mean any of that," said POPS, as he helped the General to his feet.

"I know," said Munroe, "but we still have to stop him, and deal with the consequences later." *If we can,* he added silently. "Where do you think he's headed?"

"Remember that threat assessment of the base you had us quietly conduct a couple of months ago?"

"Yes, I...NO!" said the General, as his face turned pale. "He's headed for the armory!"

"Correct. I shall stop him, while you stop Professor Tone," said POPS, before sharing his plan with the base commander.

Alex Conroy ran as fast as he could. Despite his heroic feats, super speed wasn't one of his amazing abilities. In many ways, he was still just an ordinary human being.

Conflicting thoughts raced through his mind. To destroy or not destroy the base? To be a willing slave or fight for his freedom?

During his overnight studies, thoughts of being in this situation had occurred to him. Conroy didn't consider himself immune to mind control by any stretch of the imagination, but had thought himself a more difficult subject to possess.

As opposing thoughts of defiance and obedience filled his brain, Ghost Boy heard a roaring noise and suddenly found himself no longer touching solid ground.

A convoy of military vehicles soon raced down the desert highway. Amongst them was a radio truck monitoring a specific frequency, but so far the trail had stayed consistent with the public broadcast signal of the local station that was playing in the mess hall kitchen when Ghost Boy went berserk.

In the lead jeep was General Munroe, angrily grinding an unlit cigar between clinched teeth. He had paused only long enough to obtain a new sidearm along with his self ordered ear protection, while retrieving his combat helmet before launching the mission. Further thoughts of what he would do with Professor Tone once he had the enemy in custody filled his mind.

As the jeeps and military trucks sped toward town, passing motorists observed that every man visible was armed, and presumed the soldiers were probably on their way to some training exercise. Yet why they were all wearing earmuffs in the middle of summer was a mystery.

POPS activated the jets within his metallic boots and flew off after Ghost Boy. It only took seconds for the mechanical marvel to locate Alex and literally sweep him off his feet. Conroy initially tried to break free of his captor, but after realizing their current altitude, decided to wait until they landed.

There was a quick glimpse of flying over the barbed perimeter fencing to the military base, followed by a short view of open desert, before they flew over another barbed fence. Touchdown came moments later, when POPS released Ghost Boy within the base's nearby artillery firing range. There were no drills scheduled for today, so they had the whole area to themselves. Despite how a possessed Alex had treated the General, POPS made sure Conroy had a more proper rendezvous with the ground before landing next to him.

Ghost Boy looked around and saw nothing but partially destroyed two and three dimensional targets within otherwise open land. Part of him wished he could contact Professor Tone for help, while another side of the spectral scientist hoped that whatever his artificial ally had planned worked.

"Now we can attempt to discuss this situation rationally, and restore your correct personality," said POPS, as he took a step toward Alex.

"This is my proper personality, a loyal servant of the Empire," replied Ghost Boy, as he picked up a rock off the desert floor and throw it at his opponent. POPS only response was to catch the stone in mid-air with one hand, and then crush it within his metallic fingers, pulverized dust beginning to sift through his clenched fist.

Alex just stared as POPS silently opened his hand and let the wind blow what remained of the rock away. "You don't scare me," he said defiantly.

"The purpose to which I was created is to serve and protect Alex Conroy, the being also known as Ghost Boy," POPS stated in a surprisingly calm tone of voice. "While you are still him physically, you currently are not mentally. If I fail to restore you, at least I can keep you detained where you will not be able to harm either yourself or others until Professor Tone is defeated."

"My superior cannot be defeated," shouted Ghost Boy, as he picked up the biggest piece of a spent artillery shell he could find and threw it at his self-perceived tormentor.

POPS raised his right hand and a bolt of energy emerged from its palm, destroying the shell into useless slag long before it would have ever reached him.

The mechanical marvel took another step forward, closing the gap between himself and Ghost Boy, as Alex frantically searched the area for something else to use as a weapon against the metal man.

POPS knew it was following the most logical course of action for Ghost Boy's own good. Yet somewhere within all the hardware and circuitry that composed his proton brain was a copy of David Conroy's mind. The Photosynthetic Optimal Protection Sentry knew that it was not Alex's biological father, but he had become a friend to the son of the man who created him, if not a pseudo-surrogate of sorts. Since his activation after the elder Conroy's demise at the hands of Communist agents, POPS had been Alex's constant companion. Helping him with laboratory experiments. Fighting alongside the younger man against America's enemies, or just listening to whatever was on his mind in the quiet moments at the end of a day.

By whatever terms his existence was defined, POPS was going to save Alex Conroy or die trying.

Ghost Boy stared at his enemy, beads of sweat forming on his brow, but not just from the desert heat.

*Come on POPS, figure it out!* The thought was yelled over and over again within Alex's troubled mind. *I'm doing my best to fight Professor Tone's mind control, but this is one battle I can't win without your help.*

Without warning, POPS activated his boot jets and flew towards Ghost Boy with both metallic fists extended. Their destructive potential against human flesh was staggering to contemplate. However Alex easily sidestepped the mechanical missile.

Not bothering to stop, POPS flew over to the remains of a nearby jeep. Grabbing the military vehicle while still in motion, the amazing automaton circled around. It carried the burned out husk until he was well within range of his target, and then dropped the jeep like an aerial bomb.

Alex looked on in shock, before instinct and self preservation took over. Ghost Boy ran and jumped, narrowly dodging the makeshift missile.

He rose and dusted himself off as POPS landed. "Is that the best you can do?" he asked in a taunting tone, before picking up another rock and throwing it at his foe.

Instead of destroying it, POPS stepped out of the rock's path and let it hit the remains of a decommissioned M46 Patton Tank behind him. All of the tank's personnel hatches had been removed, and the stone made a hollow, metallic sound as it struck the old weapon.

When the echo of that noise faded into nothingness, POPS calmly replied, "No. It is not," before Alex observed an amazing feat.

"We're just outside the city limits, sir," the jeep driver shouted to the General, so he could be heard over the ear protection. With that, Munroe raised his hand. The convoy pulled off to the side of the road and came to a halt.

The General jumped out of the vehicle and ran back to the mobile tracking unit. Not bothering to climb inside, he raised the back canvas flap and shouted, "Status?"

"Suspect signal is still strong and confirmed as originating from our destination, sir," yelled the technician manning the equipment inside.

"Initiate jamming procedures and prepare for combat," ordered Munroe, before returning to his jeep.

Ghost Boy stared in disbelief as POPS reached out to grab the barrel of the Patton's 90mm main gun. Artificial hands grasped the thick tubing to the point of crushing the metal, even as gears and servo-motors strained from attempting to pick up over forty tons of what was once a Korean War mobile armored weapon.

At first, despite POPS' best effort, the tank refused to move. Even though it was now nothing but a stripped out hollow body, the robotic wonder was afraid that the M46 was above his lift capacity when it finally began to leave the desert floor.

POPS felt the strain within his limbs as the M46 rose higher off the ground. His feet began creating deep impressions as the dry desert ground beneath him started to crack. The barrel of the tank's main gun was now bent some from supporting the weight of the attached vehicle. Conroy's companion calculated the odds of the main gun breaking completely off were not in its favor and increased his efforts before the barrel snapped in two.

When the vehicle achieved a ninety degree angle in relation to the ground and POPS, the weight of the tank finally started to work in his favor.

The M46 reached the zenith of its short overhead arch and began its return trip to earth with great haste. With one last heave of metallic muscles, POPS hurled it over his shoulders as hard and fast as he could.

Not thinking his enemy capable of this accomplishment until now, Conroy realized he should run, but it was too late. The Patton Tank fell behind POPS, landing on top of Ghost Boy!

"Good morning, K-FAM, the family friendly radio station where yesterday and today's hits come alive," said the disc jockey on duty as he answered the phone in a friendly voice. "What's that? You can't pick up our station on your car radio? Well, we'll be sure to get right on that," he reassured the caller, before hanging up the phone.

Then he turned to the sound engineer on duty and said in a monotone voice, "That was the tenth loss of signal complaint in less than five minutes. Alert the master. Something's wrong."

With a sickening 'crunch', the M46 Patton Tank landed on its target with deadly accuracy. The turret touched down first, caving in upon impact as the cabin interior collapsed. Cracks started to spread out across the dry ground from the epicenter of the crash site. The cabin interior collapsed as flying dust raised by the abrupt landing was picked up on a belying breeze and gently started to blow away.

"Alex?"

Silence was the only response.

"Alex?" asked POPS in a louder tone of voice.

There was still no reply.

POPS bent down to attempt picking up the tank again when Ghost Boy emerged from the wreckage, as immaterial as his code name implied.

Amazed to find himself speechless at the moment, POPS just stared at Alex.

"The answer to the question probably on your mind is I'm fine, at least for the moment," replied the young scientist. "Unfortunately, I can't risk becoming solid again until I'm completely cured, or else I'll fall under Professor Tone's devious command again."

"Otherwise, your theories concerning the possibility of being a potential mind control target were correct?" inquired POPS.

"Yes," confirmed Ghost Boy. "Becoming immaterial freed me from Professor Tone's mind control because in this state, the tertiary auditory cortex, the part of my brain that heard and comprehended the low frequency broadcast of his orders, cannot influence the rest of my mind.

"However, I was also right that while being mind controlled, my subconscious would not willingly let me phase out of sync with the rest of the world because I didn't want to risk disobeying Professor Tone by doing so," added Alex. "I don't know whether or not he knew how being immaterial would affect his process, but only by being placed in a situation where I was forced to become ghost-like could I hope to escape his commands."

"Leaving it to me to create the necessity of using that aspect of your powers. Self preservation was the greatest motivational factor available, but you had easily escaped everything up to the jeep by only utilizing your other skills."

"I assume by now General Munroe is hot on Professor Tone's trail?" inquired Ghost Boy, to which POPS replied affirmatively. "I have to stay like this, so you can't carry me. You'll have to fly on ahead and I'll float along the best I can. But one way or another, we'll rescue Professor Patterson and make Tone pay for everything he's done."

Their target was on the western side of the city. A two story building originally erected to be warehouse space just as the twentieth century began, then refurbished to house offices after the second World War. General Munroe stopped the convoy a block away from the broadcast studios of K-FAM and deployed his men to establish a secure perimeter before the local authorities started evacuating all civilians from the surrounding area.

"AMAZED TO FIND HIMSELF SPEECHLESS AT THE MOMENT, POPS JUST STARED AT ALEX."

As he looked over a city map and finalized his plans, Munroe knew the main problem facing them was that there was no way to be absolutely certain who within the radio station's headquarters, let alone any of the nearby businesses, might be an unwilling mind controlled ally of Professor Tone until they tried to take action against his assault team.

"Everyone is a suspect until proven otherwise, especially since we still have not identified the van's driver," he told his men during the pre-deployment briefing. Michael Staton, Chester Curtis, and the man known only as Professor Tone were to be apprehended on sight. Every effort was to be made to rescue Professor Patterson and protect the civilian populace during the mission.

*I've done all I can,* realized the General, as he observed the soldiers cautiously approach the radio station to start the raid.

Staton and Curtis were using the employee's lounge on the second floor of the K-FAM building as makeshift quarters, since their current employer wanted them ready to move at a moment's notice. This was understandable to a point, yet both hoodlums agreed that Professor Tone was not the easiest employer to deal with. "We've worked for some characters before," Curtis told Staton over a cup of coffee, "but this guy takes the cake."

"Yeah. Everything you do has to be so precise. You just can't go get him, say, some wiring from this place's storeroom. It has to be an exact length and width, right down to the decimal point," complained Staton, as he got up to refill the station mug he was using. "And that attitude. Always acting like he's better than everyone else. If Tone wasn't paying so well, I'd love to knock him down a peg or two."

"I know. He acts like we're just a bunch of little children who can't even breathe for ourselves without his help," added Curtis. "I just wish I knew what happened to Gould. The boss was really mad last night when that guy we kidnapped didn't wake up when he thought he should."

"Far as I know, Tone sent Joe out on another errand. Or at least, that's what he told me when I asked earlier," said Staton, as he walked toward the window, taking a sip of his new cup of coffee.

Then Curtis saw his friend drop his mug to pull his gun out of its shoulder holster.

"We've got unwanted company," shouted Staton, as he opened the old building's traditional single sash window and started firing.

The soldiers ducked for cover as their enemy fired the first shots, but they were not the intended target.

The military men looked up to catch a brief glimpse of POPS flying overhead, before he crashed through the window to confront the gunman.

"GO! GO! GO!" shouted the squad leader, as he stood up and led the charge to rush the building.

As he heard the calamity begin, Professor Tone turned to his reluctant assistant and said, "I unfortunately have no idea what the final outcome of our experiment with Ghost Boy is, but it looks like we shall have to perform the beta test on my improved method sooner than expected." Then he activated the control panel of the auxiliary broadcast booth within the K-FAM studios.

Professor Peter Patterson looked on in a state of helplessness, afraid to take a stand against his captor. He wasn't tied to a chair now, or aware of being under any mind control, but fear for the continued safety of his family kept Patterson from acting.

"Hmm," said Tone, looking over some of the control panel readouts. "It seems the military is jamming the radio station's broadcast signal. I would not be surprised to discover that they might be attempting to protect their ears as well. Wise precautions. However I always plan ahead and we do not have time for subtlety under the present circumstances," he added, while smiling at the pair of large remote speakers. Usually used when the radio station did a broadcast from somewhere outside the confines of the studio, they now sat on a carpeted riser positioned in front of the open window and aimed at the scene below.

POPS crashed through the open window, bullets ricocheting off his metallic body as he made his aerial entry. He landed directly in front of Michael Staton and reached out to grab the hoodlum's now empty handgun, which the amazing automaton then crushed within an inorganic fist. Meanwhile, Chester Curtis attempted to take out his partner's attacker with the wooden chair he was sitting in, only to discover that POPS was no ordinary opponent. The chair shattered into useless splinters as it hit the harder surface of the mechanical man's back.

"Was that really necessary?" inquired POPS, turning to face his would-be assailant. With that, Staton and Curtis tried to run. Whether to seek assistance or simply escape was a moot point to the Protection Sentry as he grabbed each man by their individual shirt collars and lifted them a good foot off the ground.

"Unless it is a contractual obligation of some sort, I fail to comprehend why you gentlemen are still assisting Professor Tone after the death of your friend," began POPS, as he looked around the employees lounge to see if there was any method available to secure his prisoners.

"What? Joe's dead?" asked Staton.

While incapable of it himself, POPS saw the look of shock upon both men's faces and quickly filled them in on the recent discovery at the gas station.

They remained silent at the conclusion of his report. At first, POPS assumed it was an emotional reaction to the news, but their next statement proved that belief inaccurate.

"For its glory, we must destroy all enemies of the Empire," Staton and Curtis said in unison. Both spoke in a lifeless, monotone voice as they started trying to attack POPS while still his prisoners.

From the street corner closest to the action, General Munroe watched his men storm into the radio station, taking a small bit of silent pride in the fact that so far only the enemy had fired any shots in a heavily civilian populated area, and those were at a target incapable of being damaged by ordinary weapon's fire. *Soon POPS and the assault team will have Tone and his unwilling minions caught in a pincher movement. Then they'll be forced to surrender,* was his assumption.

The fact that there was no sign of Alex worried Munroe, but either Conroy was on his way and had sent POPS on ahead, or else this was one operation where they would not have Ghost Boy's services available. Either way, Alex and any other victims would soon be free from outside influence.

However, it came as a great shock to the General when someone hit him from behind.

Munroe staggered, but didn't fall completely to the ground. Instinctively placing his arms out front, he landed palms first onto the street, the concrete scraping calloused flesh. With his extended body bent in an arch with only his hands and feet touching solid ground, the General turned his head as he started to rise, and was surprised to see a police man standing over him. The officer had his service revolver drawn, finger on the trigger and aimed at Munroe's head.

"For its glory, we must destroy all enemies of the Empire," the police man said in a monotone voice as the General's eyes focused on the man starting to squeeze the trigger.

Corporal Lance Ryder approached the front entrance to the K-FAM building cautiously, his men spaced out to cover each other and himself. The entry way was solid glass panels surrounding a double door set up within the otherwise solid brick wall, but there were no sentries visible.

As his men entered single file, Ryder was surprised to find the lobby completely empty, without even a guard posted at what was visible of the second floor landing to the structure's single staircase. A quick check of the building's directory mounted on the wall next to the lone elevator confirmed the fact that the radio station occupied the entire upper floor and leased out the lower level to other businesses.

Corporal Ryder started pointing to the various office doors that could be seen around them. The plan was to deploy teams to search each office and secure anyone inside until the threat on the second floor could be neutralized.

Unfortunately, the office occupants had other ideas.

They came storming out of the suites, a mixed collection of men in suits and women in feminine business attire. Most were empty handed, their fists clenched in anger. The few that actually had anything that could be considered a weapon were armed with nothing more serious than scissors or letter openers.

Yet there was no denying their intent as everyone chanted in unison.

Although POPS held them out as far as his metallic arms would allow, Staton and Curtis started pounding on his outstretched limbs with their fists. Their legs, unable to reach their target, kicked nothing but empty air.

A quick look around the employee lounge revealed no viable solution to how his prisoners could be restrained peacefully, so POPS resorted to a cruder method. With a hoodlum in each strong arm, the mechanical marvel calculated the exact amount of force and proper angles necessary before he brought the two men together heads first.

Staton and Curtis' craniums briefly made contact with a slight sound akin to a knock, then POPS separated them as each man lost consciousness within his grasp. POPS then set the hoodlums down gently on the tiled floor before he left the employee's lounge.

In the adjoining hallway, the robotic SOS agent activated his built-in communications equipment, and tracked Professor Tone's new mental command signal to K-FAM's auxiliary control room.

Secured in the knowledge that as an inorganic being, he was invulnerable to any attempt at mind control, POPS opened the door but stopped in mid-step as he processed the sight before him.

Professor Tone was standing in the middle of the room. Next to him was Peter Patterson. The kidnapped professor was willingly holding a gun to his own head.

There was a crowd of people between Ryder's unit and the access points to the upper floor. The Corporal repositioned his men so that most faced the angry mob, with a couple guarding their rear in case more mind controlled reinforcements tried to enter the building.

The barrage started with a secretary throwing the hot contents of a coffee pot at the closest soldier, before she tried to hit him over the head with the empty container. His combat helmet deflected the blow as he grabbed her wrists, ignoring the pain of his scalded flesh.

The crowd started to press in. The soldiers concentrated on the people carrying sharp objects as the most immediate threat, disarming and restraining them while doing their best to detain the others, who had to rely on sharp kicks and blows from balled fists in hopes of destroying the Empire's enemies. Although the soldiers were careful not to harm anyone, the mind controlled minions of Professor Tone didn't share that conviction.

During the struggle, an office executive accidentally knocked off a soldier's headphones. The military man quickly discovered that ear plugs alone were not enough to protect himself from the new and improved message delivery method, because the soldier pulled out his service revolver and started firing upon the rest of his unit.

Given his current position, General Munroe stared death directly in the face the best he could. He felt no fear, although wished he had a better view of the mind controlled police officer that was about to shoot him.

*I'm not going down without a fight,* thought Munroe, as he reared back and kicked out with his legs like an angry mule.

His right foot made solid contact with something, although Munroe couldn't say what.

The General acted quickly as the shot went wild, ricocheting off the pavement mere inches from his head. Munroe spun around and launched himself from the crouched position into a football style tackle to take down his unwanted opponent.

They landed on the pavement, the cop's back to the concrete street as Munroe grabbed the gun away before the man could fire again. The General then applied a quick right fist to the officer's jaw, knocking him unconscious.

Munroe used the cop's own handcuffs to secure him, before getting up to help the next closest soldier.

The military ducked for cover where they could, reluctant to return fire within the crowded lobby. One soldier clutched his shoulder while another grabbed his now injured leg.

As the man next to him clutched his stomach, Corporal Ryder yelled for a medic while launching himself at the possessed soldier. The full weight of Ryder's body slammed into his target as the Corporal reached out in a frantic bid to grab the gun.

The two men landed on the floor amidst the mind controlled mob, which just stood there and watched the soldiers fight amongst themselves, uncertain which was their new ally and who was their foe.

The rest of Ryder's unit was not idle, as they continued to either restrain the civilian combatants with handcuffs or tried to move in and help their leader as another shot rang out.

"Do not move," warned Professor Tone, "or else your country will be short one scientist. Patterson is now under my *direct* control. One word and..."

POPS stood in the open doorway to the auxiliary control room and calculated the odds of various actions. Taking his stillness as a sign of compliance, the villain continued to speak. "I know your name, but it is very unflattering. Is the designation POPS short for something else?"

"Photosynthetic Optimal Protection Sentry," replied the mechanical man tersely, trying to buy time. He had yet to arrive at a solution to the current situation that did not risk Professor Patterson suffering any form of injury.

"Interesting," said Tone, genuinely fascinated with the scientific wonder before him. "Although not within my fields of interest or expertise, I have colleagues who would pay dearly for a closer examination of you."

"That will not be logistically possible."

"Everything has a price, including human life," commented Tone coldly, while nodding at the man next to him.

Professor Patterson was still wearing the attire he had on when kidnapped yesterday afternoon. Disheveled and in need of a shave, food, and sleep; POPS' visual examination showed no outward signs of physical damage, yet Patterson was clearly nervous. Beads of cold sweat formed on his forehead, and his hand shook while he unwillingly held the gun against his own head. POPS silently determined that whatever Tone did must have been rushed and not as thorough as his past efforts. *Patterson is aware of his status, but helpless to stop it.* The expressionless look on the man's face indicated he could not save himself, and that the weapon would not be voluntarily removed until either Tone ordered Patterson to do so, or else it fell out of a dead man's hand.

"From what we have observed of your work Professor Tone, you should be commended, to a point," said POPS. His gaze never left those before him even as he kept trying to develop an answer to the current dilemma. "Your technique has positive applications available in the field of behavioral modification concerning unwanted addictions such as drugs and alcohol."

"In light of my current aspirations, I hadn't really considered the more minor possibilities," admitted Tone. "It will be nice to have some true scientific pursuits to follow after the world is mine."

"Yours?" asked POPS. "Do you not mean…"

"They are a means to an end, nothing more," revealed Tone. "Why should those with the weapons rule when it is those with intelligence that helped them achieve power in the first place? I have friends who…"

Whatever the conclusion of that statement would have been remained unsaid as a voice beside him shouted, "BOO!"

Despite all his amazing abilities, Alex Conroy couldn't fly. The best Ghost Boy could do was float like his spectral namesake, defying gravity and wind currents to eventually reach his destination.

Traveling at a much slower rate of speed than POPS, Alex had finally reached the radio station. After one quick glance to confirm the General and his men had the situation well in hand outside, Conroy entered just in time to distract Professor Tone.

As the mind control mastermind started to say "Pat…", POPS made his move. In just a few quick steps, the amazing automaton reached out and grabbed the gun away from Professor Patterson before he could react.

Tone turned at the sound of POPS crushing the gun in his metallic hand, and started to pull his own gun out. Alex watched in satisfaction as his friend flicked a finger of its free hand at the villain's forehead. The proper amount of force was applied to knock the evil professor unconscious.

As one professor fell, so did the other. POPS caught Patterson before he could hit the floor and carried him to the closest chair. "The emotional stress of the moment took its toll, but he should recover in time," was the assessment of Conroy's companion.

"Good. Now let's go about setting things right," replied Ghost Boy.

The soldiers had to fight their way across the second floor to reach this point, for every K-FAM employee encountered tried to stop them. The unit expected to find more resistance upon entering the radio station's auxiliary broadcast studio. Instead, they discovered an immaterial Ghost Boy conferring with POPS, who was hard at work doing something with the station's equipment.

"That man needs medical attention," Ghost Boy ordered the man in the lead, pointing to Patterson, "and him a prisoner detail," indicating Tone. "Then please tell General Munroe we'll need the station broadcasting again for our cure to be totally successful."

The soldier saluted and the squad left the room with the two professors.

Following Alex's instructions, POPS recorded a new subliminal message that was soon broadcast not only on the public airwaves as K-FAM was allowed back on the air, but over the speakers Tone had set up.

"Be yourselves. Ignore anything ever told to you via this method before now and never heed or obey any other subliminal messages ever again," said POPS, who played the recorded loop for a half hour, because the SOS team wanted to ensure that anyone who might have heard instructions they had not carried out yet never did so. Their plan also had the added bonus that anyone who had been mind controlled before could never be again. At least, not by Professor Tone's procedure.

"A more permanent solution will be required, in case anyone else tries to continue Tone's work," said POPS, while reporting his brief encounter with the villain before Alex arrived.

# EPILOGUE

Although he never showed any outward indication of the fact, General Munroe was relieved to see a 'normal' Alex Conroy walk out of the K-FAM building with POPS.

After a brief, private conversation to make sure Ghost Boy was okay; Munroe got right to the heart of the matter. "Other than bumps, bruises, and a lot of headaches, the civilians and our fellow law enforcement officers will be fine. Professor Patterson is being escorted back to his family, and this time I hope he takes us up on our generous offer of base accommodations. Meanwhile, the worst injuries were on our side," added the General, before reporting on the men who would be hospitalized for a while, including Corporal Lance Ryder. He had suffered a chest wound at close range while wrestling the gun away from the possessed soldier. Thankfully the bullet had missed the heart and lungs, but Ryder would be sidelined the longest out of all those under Munroe's command.

"However, we have a more serious issue that needs addressing," revealed the General, as he led his assistant director and POPS to a police car.

"Oh?" asked Ghost Boy, as he saw Professor Tone sitting in the back seat of the vehicle with his arms handcuffed behind him.

"I'll let him explain," said Munroe, as he opened the side door.

"Would somebody please let me out of here, let alone explain to me what is going on?" asked Tone. When he spoke, his voice held none of the confidence, evil intent, or even Russian accent of past conversations. In fact, Conroy thought it now had a slightly British dialect.

"Why?" asked Alex, afraid of what the answer might be.

"My name is Arthur Harrison and I have absolutely no idea why I am being held against my will," replied the prisoner. "I am a thespian of stage and screen both large and small. The last thing I remember is being in Los Angeles, auditioning for the title role of a new film: *The Diabolical Doctor Tone*. Far from the golden words of the Bard, but work is work."

When the three outside the car just stared at him in disbelief, Harrison added, "If you don't believe me, ask Ivan Savan."

"Who?" asked Alex in return.

"The director," said Harrison. "You must have him in another car. He was with me the whole time. Even drove us around scouting locations and blocking scenes."

"We'll get right back to you as soon as we can," said Munroe, before he shut the door and led the others away from the vehicle.

"What do you think?" the General asked when they were alone.

"The possibility is small, but it does exist," admitted POPS.

"We can account for everybody involved except the van's driver," revealed Munroe. "Whoever that man is has escaped custody, for the moment. This Harrison guy's story will still have to be checked out and verified, but if he's telling the truth…"

"Then he was just a front man for the *real* 'Professor Tone'," realized Alex.

"The man stayed in the background in an allegedly low level position, but was actually the mastermind behind it all?" wondered the General.

"An intelligence cabal," said Conroy.

"What was that?" asked Munroe.

"Something tells me this is far from over General," replied Ghost Boy.

*THE END  (…for now.)*

# SOME BACKGROUND

**I** was ecstatic when Ron Fortier asked me to contribute to *Ghost Boy, Volume 2*. To say the 1960s was an interesting decade is a serious understatement. Those ten years are filled with memorable examples of hope and fear existing simultaneously. Mankind strived to reach the moon before the end of the decade to honor the lost leader who inspired that dream, while a multitude of spies both real and fictitious sought to keep America safe from enemy agents.

Unfortunately, I wasn't born until 1962; so I remember very little first hand from the era of mod fashions, great music, and interesting television programs that was troubled by civil rights issues, the assassination of prominent figures, and a major war brewing on foreign shores. Therefore, I did some serious research for *The Sound of Obedience*, from the quaint reference of "the Sunday go to meeting dress" to the workings of the inner ear.

I look forward to returning to the 1960s, and Ghost Boy, sometime in the future.

**LEE HOUSTON JR. -** is the Editor-In-Chief of The Free Choice E-zine (at www.thefreechoice.info) as well as the Writer/Creator of *Hugh Monn, Private Detective* and *Alpha* the superhero from Pro Se Productions. Filling Blank Spaces, his writing blog, can be found at http://leehoustonjr. blogspot.com/ while Lee also maintains his own Amazon Author's page and a presence on both G+ and Facebook.

Super-spy and master of disguise, Miles Drake, aka Captain Action investigates the "Riddle of the Glowing Men," by writer Jim Beard. Foreign assassins are sent to kill Captain Action and though he manages to defeat them, it is their lifeless bodies that pose the greater mystery as they give off a green, glowing radiation.

Teamed with a beautiful and seductive Russian Agent, Captain Action travels to the barren, frozen wastelands of Siberia where the secret behind the glowing men lies buried in a fantastic, lost underground world. It is a secret also pursued by his most dangerous nemesis, the insidious Dr. Evil. What is this strange power hidden beneath the earth that could destroy all of mankind and who will unlock its mysteries first?

AN AIRSHIP 27 PRODUCTION
AIRSHIP27HANGAR.COM

New PULP

## PULP FICTION FOR A NEW GENERATION!
AVAILABLE AT AMAZON.COM AND AS AN EBOOK PDF AT
AIRSHIP27HANGAR.COM

# ACTION IN JAPAN!

While on assignment in Japan, Captain Action™ is haunted by the woman he loved and lost years ago in the underground kingdom beneath Siberia. When she mysteriously begins reappearing during his clandestine mission to witness a newly discovered power source, agent Miles Drake begins to question his own sanity.

Forces are at work to steal two naturally formed energy stones whose limitless power in the wrong hands could destroy the world. When he begins to suspect his alien nemesis, Dr. Evil, is behind these attacks, Drake has to utilize his most daring disguises ever to learn the truth and ally himself with an old vigilante hero from the past.

Now the one and only Captain Action must walk a delicate tightrope between old and new allies while attempting to discover the source of the threat to the Hearts of the Rising Sun. If he fails, mankind is doomed!

# THE SANDS OF FOREVER

When a top A.C.T.I.O.N. agent goes missing in the arid wastelands of the Libyan Desert, the super secret organization sends in their top field operative; Nicola Sinclair – Codename: Lady Action.

An ancient power as old as the earth lies buried there and a wealthy Arab tycoon with ties to Islamic Terrorists groups will do anything to claim it. With only a few brave allies and her considerable skills, the lovely and deadly Lady Action must defeat this powerful villain and uncover the secret of the Sands of Forever or the civilized world is doomed to destruction.

Combining the modern day flair of today's spy thrillers with the pacing of new pulp adventures, Ron Fortier brings to life one of the most charismatic new action heroes ever to dive into danger and suspense.

## PULP FICTION FOR A NEW GENERATION!

www.ingramcontent.com/pod-product-compliance
Lightning Source LLC
Chambersburg PA
CBHW071238250626
47163CB00001B/239